JANE KURTZ

Anna WAS Here

Greenwillow Books
An Imprint of HarperCollinsPublishers

Thanks to the High Test Girls for hand holding, tough feedback, and hope. Thanks, also, to LeAnn Clark and Carol Settgast, Kansas educators with passion and determination; to the smart young researchers at Sheridan Elementary School in Junction City, Kansas; and to all the churches who've shared potluck feasts with me.

Anna Was Here
Copyright © 2013 by Jane Kurtz

The text of this book is set in Berkeley Oldstyle Medium.
Book design by Sylvie Le Floc'h

Library of Congress Cataloging-in-Publication Data
Kurtz, Jane.
Anna was here / by Jane Kurtz.
p. cm.
"Greenwillow Books."
Summary: Three generations of the Nickel family reunite, when fourth-grader Anna, her mom and dad, and four-year-old sister Isabella relocate to Oakwood, Kansas.
ISBN 978-0-06-056493-3 (trade bdg.)
[1. Families—Fiction. 2. Moving, Household—Fiction. 3. City and town life—Kansas—Fiction. 4. Kansas—Fiction.] I. Title.
PZ7.K9626Le2011 [Fic]—dc22 2010017857

13 14 15 16 CG/RRDH 10 9 8 7 6 5 4 3 2 1
First Edition

 Greenwillow Books

*For all my Goering relatives
who share history, family stories,
and sweet Kansas hospitality*

∾ Contents ∾

CHAPTER 1

ꙮ

The Last Meeting
of the Safety Club

I was attending the weekly meeting of the Safety Club and thinking about my birthday party when the best thing and the worst thing of my entire life filled me up and knocked me flat.

Squish, squash, smoosh, splat.

The best thing was the bear.

It was early April, and Jericho was sitting at my desk in my perfect green bedroom. She was the college student who stayed with me after school. She had a tiny star tattoo on her shoulder and chopsticks that she used to wrap her hair into a beautiful twist.

I was pretzel legs on my pillow with Midnight H. Cat purring in my lap.

My Safety Club Notebook was open to my pyramid page, but I was thinking about my birthday party. Everybody in my class was already ten. My turn didn't come until May 27, the utter end of fourth grade.

So even though I had researched pyramid safety, I thought maybe we could plan my birthday party instead.

Pyramid or birthday?

Grandpa and Grandma Campbell liked birthday camping. If Jericho had a tent, I could invite her to come, too. That would be enough guests for me.

"Take it away, Anna." Jericho tapped her pencil on her Safety Notebook to show she was ready.

Uh-oh. Jericho was my Sunday School teacher and part of Dad's college group. She was also the only other member left of the Safety Club—besides my cat—and I didn't want to do anything that might make Jericho resign.

So *not* birthday.

I held my Safety Notebook open. "What I researched

this week is getting sealed inside a pyramid."

Jericho gave me a thumbs-up. Midnight H. Cat slid off my lap and trotted over to the window seat. Something had caught her attention. I tried not to be distracted.

"Find the king's coffin and stand facing it," I said. "The exit will be on your right. Unluckily, it will be sealed by an enormous block of granite. Luckily, you can break a stone vase and use it to carve into the limestone around the granite. You'll be in pure dark, but grope until you find a corridor and crawl along it."

Jericho gave me another thumbs-up. She and I had invented the Safety Club when everyone was feeling freaked about the wildfires roaring across Colorado last summer. Jericho said she was always braver when she felt prepared, and I said me, too.

"Use the stone blocks." I used my finger to show the route. "You'll know you're getting closer to the outside when they start getting warmer to the touch."

Jericho gasped.

Shiverydee. Had I said something wrong?

She pointed toward my cat. "Is that a bear?"

We rushed over to the window. The bear in our yard was like a walking rug—big as a car. "Yow," Jericho whispered. Midnight H. Cat switched her tail.

Luckily, the Safety Club had studied bear safety.

1. It wasn't a grizzly bear because it had no hump.

2. No one in my family was silly enough to leave food or smelly clothes outside.

3. Jericho and I were remaining calm, and since the bear was outside and we were inside, we were obviously giving it lots of room.

The bear rubbed against a tree. "The wildfires pushed animals out of their habitats and into the city," Jericho whispered. "Deer. Raccoons. Now bears."

I squinted at the faraway mountains where the bear probably belonged. The ex-members of the Safety Club would be running and screaming. It was a good thing Jericho and Midnight H. Cat and I were the only ones left.

"I'm staying calm," I whispered.

That was Plan A. It was also good to have a Plan B. If a bear charged, you could throw your camera on the ground and maybe distract it. Never run, though. Bears can run thirty miles per hour, and you can't.

The bear started to climb the tree. My face felt shivery with excitement.

Jericho put her hands on her heart. Staying calm. "The wildlife people say if bears aren't a nuisance, let them be."

Suddenly the bear swung its head around. It looked at me. Could it see through the glass? Midnight H. Cat rumbled low. I put out my fingers to rub her back. It was like I was inflated and floating in the biggest adventure of my life.

Then the bear shimmied down the trunk and shrugged away toward Foothills Park.

I let my shaky breath out. Jericho rushed back to the desk. "They'll be all over the place this summer." She grabbed her notebook.

I tucked my cat under my chin, feeling her

whiskers poke my neck. Jericho was right. Preparation did make a person brave. "That was *amazing*!" I said.

"I'll bet you won't see any bears in Kansas," Jericho said.

"What?" My hands squeezed, and Midnight H. Cat clawed me. "Ouch!" I dropped her, and she started licking herself indignantly.

Jericho looked like she had swallowed a raspberry whole. "I thought you knew." She coughed. "Your dad told us at the college group and said if he ever needed prayers, he needed them now."

I'd never seen her look so sorry.

I'd never seen my cat look so insulted.

And me?

Totally unprepared.

That's how I learned that sometimes the best and worst things come together.

Squish, squash, smoosh, splat.

CHAPTER 2
◦◦

Good-bye, House,
Be Back Soon

I sat in the backseat of the car, feeling as grumpy as a tiger salamander in sand. Dad climbed in singing, "Indoors, outdoors, in the sun."

A Beach Boys song. I could predict what rhymed with *sun*. Something I wasn't having.

Fun.

"Fun is backpacking," I said. "Fun is zip lines and seeing *bears*. Not riding in a car to Kansas."

Dad laughed.

I patted Isabella's car seat. "Back seat belt check."

Mom didn't look up from her book. "Front right check," she said.

Good. Distracted safety was better than no safety at all.

Dad hooked his arm over the drivers' seat. "Go, go, Anna Nickel, Gold Ribbon Safety Citizen." He oozed the car backward.

"Of the whole fourth grade." I thumped his arm. "And you don't have your seat belt on."

Dad swung the car onto the street and parked. Isabella leaned forward, blinking like a large owl. "Are we there?"

I groaned. Mom explained the concept—again—that we were going to be stuck in the car all day, all the way to Oakwood, Kansas. Dad got out and ran back to our porch and handed our very own keys to our very own house to Owen's mom, who was going to live here until we got back.

Tonight I wouldn't sleep in my perfect green bedroom. I would sleep in Kansas in a house that belonged to a *church*.

What a disaster.

On our porch, Owen hung his chin over the railing. His mom used to play her guitar with Dad in church and say, "Let us lift our voices in joyful song." A few months ago she made us sing something achy sad about the rivers of Babylon and I predicted she was getting a divorce, and she was.

I felt bad for her. I really did! But why did Dad have to get the noble idea to loan her *our* house and our furniture? My knee skin was still stuck to the porch from the time I tripped over my wheeled shoes and fell flat. I never thought I'd have to say good-bye to my skin. Or to Miranda's grave.

Miranda had a lacy dress and gloves that came up to her elbows. She had eyes like blue almonds. When the neighbor's Great Dane chewed up Miranda, Dad helped me dig a grave under the dogwood where petals fell on it. We sang "Abide with Me," and I wept.

I never did forgive that dog, even though Jericho said forgiveness was very important.

Dad leaned on the porch rail. All sympathetic!

He'd better tell Owen's mom not to get used to our house because we'd be coming back *soon*.

Last night in my perfect green room, I got up and turned on the closet light. Then I wrote on my closet wall, "Anna was here." After a minute, I wrote, "And she'll be back."

But when?

Now I watched Dad shake hands with Owen. Dad believes in good karma and peacemaking. He says, "Actions speak louder than words" and "Never give up hope."

I peered under the seat, trying to see my cat. She had a perfectly good cat carrier—beside me on the seat—but she refused to come out. Dad's car door opened. "Let's rock and roll," he said. "Take one last look around."

I considered pointing out that in the Bible when Lot's wife looked back, she turned into a pillar of salt. A few minutes later the car rumbled forward.

"Stop," Isabella said. "We need to twist in the swings in the park."

Mom explained the concept of finding twisty swings in Kansas. I hugged my ankles and bumped my head purposely on the seat.

"Got a plan back there?" Dad asked.

My plan was to stay folded up. Mom and Dad could see how they liked having a daughter who looked like a lawn chair in a garage.

The car went faster. Midnight H. Cat squeaked. I stretched my fingers out. Her fur felt soft and scared.

Turn around, I thought.

If Dad turned around, we could be in the mountains in an hour. We'd set up tents, and Grandpa Campbell would tell his favorite story about when Mom was a girl and a moose trotted around the campground with her pajamas in its mouth.

This direction?

We'd never had any reason to go east.

Now I knew what a tiger salamander and Midnight H. Cat and Anna Nickel had in common.

They don't like to change their habitat.

CHAPTER 3

෬

When Did Dad
Turn into Moses?

On the day of the bear, I made Jericho tell me everything she knew. "Not much," she said. "A church in Oakwood, Kansas, is having problems. Your dad hopes he can get them over the hump."

Dad sometimes said, "My roots are in Oakwood, Kansas." It made me imagine him as a big Colorado tree with roots shooting out sideways into the next state. But he hadn't been in Oakwood since he was a kid. And I didn't understand—and no one still had explained to me—how churches got humps or how long it took to get over one or how Dad could help. He wasn't even a preaching-every-Sunday-in-charge-of-everything   kind of minister.

I felt the car slow down. Stop sign, I predicted. Last summer, when Jericho and I made an evacuation plan, she and Midnight H. Cat and I walked around these blocks and counted the steps in case I had to find my way in the dark.

The car eased forward again. A garbage truck groaned. With a few turns, we could be at my school. I'd rush down the hall past the fourth-grade safety display with my gold ribbon on my hurricane poster . . . only it was too early. No one would be in my classroom yet except the tiger salamander.

"Stop," Isabella said. "We need to pet the cow."

We must be passing her preschool with the painted cow in the yard. If we turned right, we'd be at the church. Jericho and I walked to Dad's church almost every afternoon and read Dad's name on the sign beside CONTEMPORARY SERVICE IN THE CHAPEL—"START SMALL."

On the day of the bear I'd asked, "Why?"

"Our church has four ministers," Jericho said.

"The Oakwood church has zero. He probably thought it was fair to share. Didn't his mom grow up in Oakwood?"

"Right." But she moved to California. By the time Dad was in college, both his parents had died, and then he'd met Mom, and her family had scooped him in.

Outside, someone called, "Got time for coffee?" The city was waking up. In a few minutes we'd pass the high school where Mom had taken AP history and decided she'd become a college history professor.

Beyond that?

We never went beyond that.

Turn around, I thought desperately. In the Bible an angel made a donkey speak up and tell Balaam to turn around. I needed an angel and a donkey like that on my team.

Instead, the car sped up and city sounds melted away.

Why, why, why? drummed in my head. *How long, how long?*

The day of the bear Dad apologized at supper for sharing the news with the college group before telling

Isabella and me. Then he said, "When I read the letter from the church, I think I heard a call."

"The call of God?" I tried to see if he was starting to sprout a beard like Moses in the picture in my third-grade Bible.

Mom said, "Wouldn't it be handy if God sent important messages on a banner behind an airplane, so everyone can read them?"

Dad said the call didn't come in a burning bush, like the call of Moses. It wasn't out loud but more like a still, small voice in the fog. He said, "It's hard for a church in a small town to find a minister. They'll have a better shot if they get over the hump."

"How long will that take?" I asked.

"Possibly not long at all." He looked like the picture in my Bible of Daniel walking boldly into the lions' den.

"All I ask," Mom said then, "is three hours a day of writing time for my journal article."

All I ask, I thought now, *is someone to tell me how long it takes to get over a hump.*

I walked my fingers to my backpack and pulled out the water bottle and Isabella's dollhouse pan. *Be prepared.* I poured the water and pushed the pan under the seat and listened for lapping sounds.

What could I do to make Midnight H. Cat less miserable?

In a sermon about Dr. Martin Luther King, Jr., Dad said when we're feeling mighty and proud, we conveniently forget God's special heart for the weak and meek. Maybe I could tear a piece of paper out of my Safety Notebook and make a peaceful protest sign—SAVE THE WEAK AND MEEK CAT—and hold it up in the car window.

Smack. Smack. Uh-oh. Isabella. Sucking her thumb. She was four and never sucked her thumb anymore.

I popped straight up. "Somebody's suffering back here!" I hollered.

Dad used the rearview mirror to lock his eyes with my eyes.

Uh-oh.

He cleared his throat. "Anna . . ."

It's bad enough when your dad puts on his preacher's voice in church.

Distract him. Quick. "Look." I pointed out the window. "Um . . . grass."

CHAPTER 4

⁀

I Refuse
to Be Dorothy

East, I discovered, was Highway 24—with no huge red rocks that looked like a ship's prow or camels kissing, with no mountains, with zero tourists. East had one thing, I pointed out.

Grass.

"It's not like we're stuck in a covered wagon," Mom said. "It's not like we're heading off to live in a soddy with cows walking on the roof."

"Look, Isabella," Dad said. "A real cow." But Isabella had gotten up too early and had thumb-sucked herself to sleep.

At Limon we got on I-70. For a while Mom entertained me with pioneer stories about buffalo stampedes and hailstones as big as eggs. "Pioneers wrote in their journals about crossing an ocean of grass," she said. "One used the prairie wind to sail his wagon across the ocean of grass until he smashed."

If Mom weren't a history professor, I'd be sure that was a made-up story.

"Ah, the ocean!" Dad said. "When I visited Oakwood, Kansas, I taught my cousins Beach Boys songs." Dad loves singing Beach Boys songs almost as much as he loves preaching about how Gandhi and Dr. Martin Luther King, Jr., used peaceful protest to challenge the mighty and the proud.

Mom smiled back at me over her glasses. "You'll have cousins!"

Cousins. A line of kids popped into my brain. They looked like Dad. They stared at me with interest and a bit of awe. Maybe I could start an Oakwood chapter of the Safety Club.

"What kind of disasters do people prepare for in

Kansas?" I asked. "Besides tornadoes. Because Jericho and I have that one down flat."

"There's my girl," Dad said. "There ain't no flies on Anna. Keep your eyes open and your game face on. Maybe you'll see some clues."

The clues were grass, cows, and one tree with fishbone branches.

At lunchtime we exited onto a small road where a picnic table sat in the middle of grass. The picnic was a disaster, though. Isabella kept saying no to all four food groups, and Midnight H. Cat still refused to get into her carrier. "She'll be fine," Mom said.

"But what about her litter box?"

"She'll hold it until she feels better," Dad said. "Let's keep her out of the way of rattlesnakes."

He was kidding, but I decided to finish my sandwich in the car.

The first hour after lunch Dad entertained Isabella with luckily-unluckily stories. Unluckily, a man fell out of an airplane. Luckily, there was a haystack right below him. Unluckily, the haystack had a pitchfork in it. Luckily, he missed the pitchfork. Unluckily, he missed the haystack. Dad filled up the car with what Mom and I call his rhinoceros laugh.

Just then I saw a wolf on a bluff staring down at our car. A clue? My stomach went bump-bump before I realized it was made of wood. "Are there any wolves in Kansas?" I asked.

"I hear there are feral hogs," Mom said. "Domestic hogs gone wild and threatening crops and pets."

Wow. Maybe kids in Kansas wouldn't fool around in the Safety Club like the ex-members in Colorado had. I closed my eyes and imagined I was with Jericho in my perfect green bedroom.

When Isabella yelped, my eyes popped back open. Two horses were rippling up a hill toward clouds so dark the sky looked ready to crash down on them. The radio crackled. "We apologize for the interruption. The National Weather Service has issued a tornado watch for the following—" A blast of static cut the voice off.

Shiverydee. When I was six, we watched *The*

Wizard of Oz, and as the tornado swirled Dorothy and Toto into the sky, I practically had to staple my eyes open. Now Mom squeezed Dad's arm. "Go for the ditch? Or stay in the car?"

"Maintain cool, everyone." Dad pushed a radio button, and I heard a twanging guitar. He pushed another. "Hurry in, folks, and—"

"Maybe drive into a ditch *in* the car?" Mom asked.

I flipped open my Safety Notebook.

"It's only a watch," Dad said cheerfully. "Not a warning."

"Micah Nickel!" Mom gave him one of her famous looks. Dad promptly took the next exit and parked in front of a café. The minute we got inside, rain started beating up the street outside. All the people—luckily—kept talking and clinking spoons.

"Guess I was being silly," Mom said. After we got our food, she and Dad used the alphabet noodles in Isabella's soup to make up words.

Not me. I was too busy listening to the people at the next table talk about a Chihuahua that got picked up last month by seventy-mile-an-hour winds. "Tossed her," a man said. "They found that pup a mile away."

"Yep." The woman beside him stirred her coffee with a clink-clink. "Pet psychic. I hear that psychic guided them right to her."

"Going to eat your hamburger?" Dad asked me.

Nope. If there *was* a tornado and the car lifted into the air and started twirling around, I was going to run outside so fast I would definitely see where Midnight H. Cat landed.

CHAPTER 5
ര๛

Tornado Preparation
Makes You Brave

<u>Safety Tips for Tornadoes</u>

1. Run, duck, and cover.

2. Curl into a ball.

3. Clasp your hands together behind your head to block flying stuff.

4. Get under a sturdy piece of furniture.

5. Stay away from windows because glass can fly at 320 miles per hour.

Seeing the car wheels stay on the pavement filled me with what Jericho called Gratitude Attitude. The waitress came over. "Not hungry?" She picked up my plate. "I have some nice cupcakes with pink frosting."

"Anna doesn't like pink," Isabella told her.

I couldn't even talk. Too full of Gratitude Attitude.

If you change your attitude, Jericho said, you can change the world. When the car was sailing down I-70 again, I bent over and tried stretching my mouth into a smile to see if Gratitude Attitude could change my cat's world or at least coax her into her carrier.

"All right, fellow travelers," Dad said. "*That* was interesting. But tornado watches mostly turn into nothing."

"What about the ones that don't?" Mom asked.

Dad laughed, even though Mom definitely wasn't making a joke. He said most Kansas tornadoes touch down in prairie grass. "My mother lived for nineteen years on a farm near Oakwood and saw one only once."

"Really?" I said. "She saw a tornado?"

"An aunt came to visit with her new baby," Dad said. "The cousins were chasing each other in a pasture when Mom saw a black pencil line drop out of a cloud."

"This," I said, "is a terrible story."

"No," Dad said. "They were *prepared*. Everyone clattered downstairs into the basement. While they were sitting there, they realized they'd forgotten the baby."

"They forgot the baby?" Mom gave him the famous look.

"Well, it hadn't been around long," Dad said. "It was fast asleep. My point is the tornado hopped right over the farm."

But what if it hadn't? I imagined that baby howling as it spun up and up.

"Ten kids," Mom said. "What an experiment this is going to be."

Dad grinned at her. "It'll be interesting. Get ready to be related to half the population of Oakwood. A gaggle of Stucky aunts and uncles and cousins once and twice and three times removed. All of them watching us!"

"Why will they be watching us?" I asked.

"In a small church people sometimes judge a minister by his family," Mom said. "We need to help Dad get off on the right foot."

"That sounds kind of scary," I said. "Scary is not interesting."

"Bears are scary," Isabella told me. "But not to you."

I gave her a fist bump. Isabella was the official fan of the Safety Club.

"Spiders are scary," Isabella said. "Why did God have to make spiders?"

"If we didn't have spiders, bugs would take over the world." Dad made a shivery noise. "We wouldn't want mosquitoes everywhere, would we? Fate worse than death."

"What about sharks?" Isabella asked.

Without sharks I guess fish would take over the world. That didn't seem like a fate worse than death.

All the long afternoon, as we drove with one quick stop for supper, I wondered about things. Did the Oakwood fourth graders have a tiger salamander? Had they studied caterpillar legs and prolegs? Had they made disaster posters?

I also discussed earthquakes with Dad and reviewed my Safety Notebook.

Anna Nickel, Gold Ribbon Safety Citizen of the whole fourth grade, was going to be ready for anything.

CHAPTER 6

怣

Grandma Didn't Stick
and I Won't Either

We drove and drove—for seven hours and forty minutes. Isabella said, "Are we there?" about 740 times. My cat carrier bounced along empty because my cat stayed under the seat. "Good thing we never drove to Oakwood before," I said. "People have been known to die in captivity, you know."

Mom's glasses glinted in the dusk. "If you ever get thrown into a prison of solid stone, you can survive by soaking rags in the water that seeps in."

"Also, prisoners have been known to survive by keeping their minds hopeful." That was Dad.

"Here's something for your notebook," Mom said. "If you get chained to a wall, push against your bonds and then relax. It keeps blood flowing to your fingers. And grasshoppers and beetles and termites are all good sources of protein. Avoid cockroaches and rats, though. Too much bacteria."

Unsavory. "Why didn't *we* ever come to Oakwood for vacation?" I asked.

Mom glanced at Dad.

"What?" I said.

Mom reached over and squeezed Dad's shoulder.

"What?" I said.

Isabella smack-smacked her thumb. "Well," Mom said, "in Dad's family, people mostly stuck tight in Oakwood. His mom didn't."

Dad's mom had become an angel so long ago. I imagined an unsticky angel bouncing from cloud to cloud. Dad rubbed his neck. "Mom used to say the only thing dumber than a turkey is the farmer who tries to raise it."

The line of kids popped back into my brain—with

farmer hats and straw sticking out of their mouths. "So I have a bunch of turkey-raising farmer cousins?"

Dad was quiet. I stared out where the low sun made the grass look like a fuzzy carpet and the oil pumps look like dark grasshoppers. "My mom sold her acres," he said finally. "Her brothers and sisters gave up on farming then. Aunt Lydia hung on to the house and a few rocky, hilly acres."

No farmer cousins. I felt strangely disappointed.

"I hear my cousin Caroline has quit being a cop to try to farm those old acres. Probably doomed for failure, though." Dad pointed out the window. "These days Kansas has wind farms."

I looked out at the giant white arms slowly turning. In my mind, someone named Cousin Caroline ran under them with a huge net, harvesting wind.

"Stinky," Isabella said. Two seconds later we passed a truck with holes in the side. Through the holes I could see eyes and tails.

I imagined Oakwood fourth graders sitting around me at lunch. I could say, "Cows and turkeys? I saw a *bear*." I tapped Mom's shoulder. "Don't you think the Oakwood school will be awfully small for me?"

"It will be exactly the right size for you," Mom and Dad said in unison. They thought it was perfect that I would have four weeks in school to meet other kids before summer vacation.

"Stinky," Isabella said again. I looked out at red flickering in the dusk. Dad said some farmer lit a fire on purpose to kill the weeds and because the ash serves as fertilizer. I held my nose and shivered.

Too much like the smell of wildfires last July.

"Getting close!" Dad took the next exit and let out a big cheer and instantly got stuck behind a tractor clogging up the road.

Mom unfolded the church's letter about the house. "Watch for Cole Street."

I squinted out the window. In a clearing next to the road was a wooden horse with its head hanging down and a cut-out wooden cowboy kneeling next to it.

The tractor turned onto a side road, and Dad sped up.

Ahead I got a quick glimpse of lights. Then the

road dipped. "Welcome to Oakwood," Mom said, pointing to a sign. "And look. We're on Cole Street."

We drove to the *only* house on Cole Street. I saw a tree with a branch stretching out toward the street. In Colorado we didn't have any good climbing trees, which was a waste of good muscles since I could do the third most pull-ups of the kids in fourth grade.

Dad pulled into the driveway and stopped.

"Be careful," I said. "Don't let Midnight H. Cat escape." I cracked the car door open. The porch light was on, and something in the yard buzzed loudly—too steady to be a rattlesnake, I hoped. I went around and helped Isabella out. She grabbed me tight around the neck. "Carry me."

"No way. You're *huge*."

She uncurled her hand. "Want my lucky jelly bean?"

"Thanks." I set her down and popped it into my mouth. "What makes it lucky?"

"I licked it," she said.

When she wasn't looking, I spit it into the grass. I probably needed some good luck here in Oakwood, Kansas, but not *that* much.

CHAPTER 7

⌒

Pink Stinks

The church's house was definitely not a soddy. It was a two-story and made of wood. Mom came up beside me. "Hello to our temporary home." She gave me a squeeze.

I got my backpack and coaxed and pulled Midnight H. Cat from under the seat. When I lifted her into the evening air, she squirmed to let me know I was holding her too tightly.

"Carry me," Isabella told Dad.

Dad handed our sleeping bags to Mom and swung Isabella up. Lucky duck. Even though I knew better, my brain wanted to be walking toward *my* house. My skin. My perfect green room.

"The church is right down the street," Dad said.

We climbed onto the porch. Mom dug the key out of Dad's pocket and unlocked the door. I pushed it open and plopped my cat inside. She dashed forward. "Wait!" I shouted.

"She'll be fine," Dad told me.

"What if she's not?

"She will be."

Mom turned on a light. Big flowery couch. Living room chairs. I could smell a faint bad egg smell I knew from camping at hot springs was sulfur.

"We should get some sleep." Mom's short hair was sticking up, and she took off her glasses and rubbed her eyes. "Isabella's almost out. Sure is hot in here."

Isabella's head had flopped on Dad's shoulder. "Follow me," he whispered.

I took two sleeping bags from Mom, and we all squeaked up the stairs. Another hall. "Ta-da." Dad pushed open a door, and I saw the glow of a night-light. He cleared his throat.

I peeked in. Pink. "This better not be my room."

Dad cleared his throat again. "Nice of the building and grounds committee to think of new paint," he said.

"There are other bedrooms," I said. "There have to be."

"Maintain cool, Anna," Dad whispered.

We crossed to a tiny bedroom with elephants on the wall in a night-light glow. Dad laid Isabella down on the small bed. Mom said, "Look, the bed's made. How thoughtful."

I opened the connecting door. Big bed. Big dresser. Mom and Dad's room.

Suddenly I was too tired to maintain cool. "This is unjust," I said. "Why didn't that committee ask me what color I wanted my room to be? And why did they even bother to repaint when we're only going to be here a little while?"

"Honey," Mom said, "we've been in a car all day. . . ."

"And Aunt Dorcas Stucky, one of my mother's sisters, is coming over early." Dad put his arms around me, sleeping bags and all. "I hope she isn't too old and weak to help with the unpacking. You two go to bed, and I'll bring our things in."

"Don't accidentally let the cat out." My voice was sandy in my throat. "She can be tricky."

Mom kissed me. "Dad can outtrick any cat."

"I'll set up the litter box and put the carrier in the living room with its door open." Dad shoulder-walked me to the pink room. "Maybe she'll feel safer in her carrier."

He kissed me good-night, took one of the sleeping bags, and squeaked back downstairs. I dropped the other sleeping bag in the corner and stood looking out the window, wishing it faced the big tree. My body felt like it was still in the car, rumbling along, and my brain was back in that café.

I had a stomach-looping feeling even the Safety Club hadn't taught me enough to be prepared for Kansas.

CHAPTER 8

Even a Small Miracle
Is a Good Miracle

I squinted out, trying to see the sky. *What if?* seemed more real in the dark. Did tornadoes ever come at night? Dad's footsteps squeaked on the stairs. "Daddy," Isabella called sleepily.

"What?"

"I think I see a spider."

What happened to spiders in tornadoes? Did they whirl up and up, trying frantically to spin a web?

Dad walked down the hall to Isabella's room. I waited until he walked back. "Dad," I called.

Dad made a kind of *mfff* sound, but he never really did get mad.

"What kind of safety warning system does Oakwood have?" I asked.

"A siren. We'd all hear it. Go to sleep, please."

I sat on the bed like a stick with wide-open eyes, listening, the way Midnight listens when her ears go forward and the rest of her stays massively still. Was that a siren? Or just a car horn?

I got up and groped in my backpack until I found my Safety Notebook. Back on the bed, I squeezed it tightly.

Plan A, I thought. *Plan B.* Even those words made me feel better. Now where was my cat?

Dad was coming upstairs again. I quickly put my sleeping game face on. The door opened. I peeked at Dad lugging my suitcase in. I didn't say anything, though. He would be proud if I could get to sleep.

When he was gone, I opened my eyes again and studied the shadows on the ceiling.

On the night when wildfires raced through the city and our house filled up with the college students from

Dad's church group, Jericho had been calm. She showed me her plan. She asked Dad if he would pray with them.

Dad was always being asked to pray. "Nothing special about a minister's prayers," he'd say. "All God's children are equal pray-ers in the sight of God." Still, he always did it. That made people like me a little out of practice.

But it was a good idea to get God on my team.

I closed my eyes. *Dear God. I need my cat. Also please help Dad get the church over the hump quickly so we can go back to Colorado soon. Preferably by my birthday.* I opened my eyes. I did realize my birthday was in five weeks. But still.

God could work miracles.

Should I have knelt and folded my hands? No. Jericho said God heard prayers anywhere and anytime. But she said it was wrong to expect God to do everything.

I closed my eyes again. *P.S. I promise to do my part. Amen.* Even Dad sometimes said "P.S." But what was my part, exactly?

Don't be evil and insincere. I knew that much.

Some people said God wanted everything: our hearts, our minds, and all the efforts of our hands, which seemed kind of drastic.

I sat completely still and waited to feel something. *P.P.S.* I thought. *Please give me a sign that you heard.*

Finally I opened my eyes. It was darker now. Dad must have turned off the porch light. I wished I could look for Midnight. Instead, I crawled over and found my sleeping bag and spread it out on the bed. There. The sleeping bag smelled like home. The sleeping bag said "temporary."

I thought about Great-aunt Dorcas coming early. Would she bring cousins? I squeezed my eyes tight. People were always better prepared when they had a good night's sleep. But how could I sleep without my cat?

Then I heard light, pittery feet.

Basically a miracle.

I took off my socks and rolled them into a sock ball and threw it as hard as I could. Midnight H.

Cat tore after the ball. I giggled.

Suddenly I was full of good cheer. I didn't even have to sleep in a pink room if I didn't want to. I dragged my sleeping bag into the hall and wiggled into it. Midnight curled up on my long hair, purring.

Kids who said cats couldn't retrieve things were flat out wrong. Kids who said cats freaked out when you took them to a new place could be wrong, too.

All was calm. All was bright.

CHAPTER 9

∽

Totally Unprepared

A moderate earthquake in the Humboldt Fault Zone could turn the sand under Tuttle Creek Dam to quicksand and cause a flood. Dad says the Humboldt Fault Zone isn't close enough to Oakwood to lose any sleep over it. I say . . .

Safety Tips for Earthquakes

1. Look for something sturdy.

2. Drop.

3. Cover.

4. Hold on.

The first morning in Oakwood, Kansas, I opened my eyes and saw that I was back inside the pink room. I got up and went over to my suitcase. A booklet was lying on it: *Kansas Safety Tips*.

Dad was the best.

The picture on the front showed a tornado vacuuming up everything. Our class this year had made a wall display with natural disasters of the world. I knew the eye of a hurricane could be up to fifty feet high and twenty to thirty miles wide, and a fourth grader could make a great picture of a hurricane by using cotton balls.

I opened the booklet and read a little bit. *Kansas Safety Tips* made me feel ready for adventure. I got dressed and went into the hall.

At the top of the stairs I saw a guy walk by in the living room carrying a box. Our furniture had stayed in Colorado, but Mom and Dad needed their books.

I tiptoed down and slipped out the front door to check out that tree. Good thing I was alone—in case I wasn't as good at climbing as I thought.

I walked over to the rough, big trunk, curled my hands around the perfect branch, and pulled. Whoosh. Up. For a few seconds I wobbled, feeling the humid air around me. Then I tipped back and hung by my knees.

Whee. My hair sailed around me. Sky. Grass. Tree.

I maneuvered myself upright again and climbed into the branches, high enough to see a grassy field between us and the church.

This house was on the edge of town. Across Cole Street, I could see a creek and then the roofs of other houses not far away, which meant there'd be a park with twisty swings for Isabella and kids I could vote into the Oakwood Safety Club.

A squeaking. A boy. Coming down the street on a red bicycle. "Hey," I shouted.

He put his head down and pedaled faster.

I wasn't actually prepared for that.

The house door slammed. Dad shook hands with the box delivery guy, who climbed into his truck and rumbled off. Minutes later a car came down Cole Street and turned into our driveway.

A person who had to be Great-aunt Dorcas got out. No cousins. Just a woman with stern hair and a sunflower dress and a big bowl. I had better stay camouflaged for now.

Dad walked up to her, and she gave him the bowl and took his face in her hands. "Micah Nickel," she said. "You look exactly like your mother."

Grandma must have been very tall and her hair must have been very short. I tried not to giggle.

The woman took Dad's arm. "Did you bring this heat with you?"

If Great-aunt Dorcas was old and weak, I was a sweet potato. And if she thought we brought heat, she didn't know Colorado.

"I was sorry to hear about Uncle Jacob," Dad said.

"We shall meet on that beautiful shore. I've moved in with Lydia." She steered Dad on the porch. "My dear sister is not long for this world either, I'm afraid. Caroline is back." Great-aunt Dorcas made a disapproving noise. "I told her it was simply silly to think she can farm those—" Great-aunt Dorcas swept Dad inside.

My stomach growled.

Squeak. The boy on the red bicycle. Coming toward me again. Third grader, I predicted.

I scooched farther out on the branch toward Cole Street. "Hey," I called again.

He looked up—like a feral hog about to charge. "Preacher's kid!" he shouted.

Maintain cool.

That's what I was thinking until the water balloon exploded right in my face.

CHAPTER 10

⤜⤏

Live by the Sword,
Cry by the Sword

I blinked water out of my eyes and swung down from the tree. I grabbed a stick and held it out like Moses. "I smite you," I hollered as he rode away.

What was wrong with that kid anyway?

If Dad had heard me, he would have said that smiting was living by the sword and the problem with living by the sword was dying by the sword. I marched into the house, using my shirt to wipe my face and neck.

Dad was a peacemaker. If he had been around when Samson was alive, he would have pointed out that Samson should try a little negotiation with the

Philistines instead of sending foxes with burning tails into the Philistines' fields. Still, I needed his help.

I hurried past a stack of boxes. In the next room was a table piled with casserole dishes and plates covered with plastic wrap. Great-aunt Dorcas's voice blared out. "Mercy, Micah! The Budget and Finance Committee won't take it well if you're late."

A door swung open, and Dad rushed through. I pretty much tackled him. "Dad . . ."

He slid me off. "Be helpful to Mom, okay? We'll wait for tomorrow to enroll you in school. Why is your shirt damp?" He didn't wait for answers.

Outrageous!

He hurried out the front door. I shut it tightly behind him, went up to change my shirt, and came back down to see if I'd have more luck talking to Mom.

I peeked into the kitchen and saw Isabella hanging on to Mom's leg. Great-aunt Dorcas was saying, "You'll feel better, dear, once we get those casseroles into the freezer."

Uh-oh. What Great-aunt Dorcas obviously didn't

know was that Mom would feel better only when her *books* were put away.

Great-aunt Dorcas opened a drawer and murmured, "Mercy, mercy." She pulled out a handful of spoons.

I stepped into the kitchen. "Can I visit Dad?"

Great-aunt Dorcas gave Mom a head shake. "Believe me. If Micah gets off on the right foot with the Budget and Finance Committee, it will be a blessing." She waved the silverware. "Anna can give these spoons a good scrub."

"Anna," Mom said, "please introduce yourself to Great-aunt Dorcas officially and politely."

Great-aunt Dorcas turned. I was going to explain how much Dad liked having visits from me. I was going to explain that the spoons were perfectly clean enough for Mom and for me. But I knew from my great-aunt's expression she would definitely have her own opinion.

As I saw her gaze go around the kitchen, I also knew she was seeing other things that needed a good scrub.

Right then I felt *exactly* like our classroom caterpillars must have felt—trapped in a big cage with no way out.

CHAPTER 11
୶

The Angel

After I officially and politely met Great-aunt Dorcas, I officially and politely asked Mom if she would like me to baby-sit Isabella. I felt sorry to leave Mom with Great-aunt Dorcas. I really did! But I had to get out of there as fast as my legs and prolegs would go.

Isabella and I got one oatmeal cookie each from a plate on the table. Oatmeal cookies were practically the same as granola.

As we ate on the porch, I checked to see if Isabella remembered *stop, drop,* and *roll*. Then we practiced *run, duck,* and *cover,* which was for tornadoes.

"Now," I told her, "let's get to work on the new safety plan."

Back inside, where Mom and Great-aunt Dorcas had unfortunately taken the cookie plates away, we found the basement. At the bottom of the steps sat Midnight H. Cat. "Is this a safe place?" I asked her. "What do your cat instincts tell you?"

She rubbed against my ankle, which I thought meant yes. "First we need emergency supplies," I told Isabella.

Upstairs we opened closets until we found blankets. I counted out four, and we carried them into the basement. "We need canned goods," I said. "And water in a jug." Did water ever go stale?

Isabella and I practiced the steps to the basement with our eyes closed in case the lights got knocked out. "Want to walk over to the church and see if Dad has a flashlight?" I asked.

"Can we?" Isabella asked as I led her outside. "Is it safe?"

I considered. I hadn't made any plans for being

attacked. But the mean kid should be in school by now. I hopped onto the sidewalk and back onto our grass. "Look. Nothing scary."

"How will we know our way back?" Isabella asked.

"We could throw bread crumbs. Like Hansel and Gretel."

Isabella sniffled. "The witch put Hansel in the oven."

I was sorry I had brought up Hansel and Gretel. "Come on. Dad is straight ahead with no turns."

As we got close, I showed Isabella sheep in the stained glass window. I read her the sign by the parking lot where Cole Street met up with Sycamore Street. POTLUCK WITH PIE! HELP US WELCOME OUR NEW PASTOR AND HIS FAMILY.

"That's us," Isabella said. "Do I like pie?"

I had gotten distracted by the other side of the sign. HOW MUCH IS SEVENTY TIMES SEVEN? Someone was trying to plant a mystery that might make people curious so they would come to church. Most people liked mysteries, although not me.

From here I could see plenty of yards and houses. About 5,000 people lived here, according to Dad, and I hoped 4,999 of them weren't mean.

A church door opened, and Dad came out—all frowny face. I glimpsed people behind him. Maybe the committee. Maybe people who would hold it against Dad if we interrupted. "We'll ask about the flashlight later," I said, and hustled us out of there before Isabella could say something loud.

By the time we reached the field, I was thinking of how proud Mom would be that we hadn't interrupted and also that in Colorado everyone thought Dad was fun and funny and perfect—and I never thought anyone would think otherwise—when something shot up from behind a line of trees. "Duck and cover!" I shouted, flinging Isabella down and myself over her.

Whoosh. Then silence. I tried to remember what I'd seen, but the brightness of the sun had washed out everything except long, gangly legs and huge, flapping wings.

Wow.

An angel? Every Christmas we had a church play and some kid played Angel Gabriel bringing good news of great joy.

We ran the rest of the way to the house. Great-aunt Dorcas and Mom were standing at the bottom of the steps, and Isabella headed straight for Mom's knees. "You get some rest," Great-aunt Dorcas was saying. "People will want to chitchat and say their welcomes."

"Wonderful," said Mom faintly. "You could let them know—"

Great-aunt Dorcas nodded. "They know you need a day or two to catch your breath."

Mom ran a hand through her sweaty hair, and it stood up in spikes. In Colorado, people knew she wasn't big on chitchat or potlucks. I was feeling sorry for her when Great-aunt Dorcas said, "Why don't I help you out and take Anna with me to the farm for a few hours?"

"No," I mouthed to Mom behind Great-aunt Dorcas's back.

"She'll be a help with the pies." Great-aunt Dorcas reached for my arm. "I'll never forgive myself if we run out at the potluck."

Mom said, "That's kind—"

Nononono.

"These old hands are not what they used to be." Great-aunt Dorcas was steering me toward the car now.

"Well," Mom said, "if you need the help . . ."

I wondered what Great-aunt Dorcas's hands *used* to be. "No, thank you," I said.

I said it nicely. Even so, next thing I knew, I was sitting in the front seat of Great-aunt Dorcas's car with my seat belt on, listening to her say the ants were getting her rhubarb this year but last year's apples would do nicely if we skinned them.

Abduction! *Dad! Jericho,* I shouted in my mind. *Help!*

CHAPTER 12

ↄↄ

Meeting the Great-Aunts

The car rolled past the Oakwood sign and out of town. Dad popped into my brain. "Maintain cool. She's your great-aunt," he said. Jericho popped in behind him. "Be brave and look for opportunity," she said.

The car rolled past the mysterious wooden horse and cowboy kneeling by the side of the road. I took a deep breath. "Do you by any chance happen to know who could have ridden a bicycle by our house before breakfast?" I glanced at Great-aunt Dorcas out of the corner of my eye. "A kid, I mean? By himself?"

"Red bicycle?" She gave me a pinch-mouth look.

"What has Simon Stucky done this time?"

Stucky? "So he's *related* to me?"

"His grandfather was my brother." She launched in—and it didn't sound like a short story. "He was born four years after Lydia, when our parents were helping with the old Miller place and . . ."

Eventually I tuned out and started making up my own predictions. Had my grandma and Simon's grandpa maybe started some ancient family feud?

Now Great-aunt Dorcas was talking about how Simon's grandpa became a bank president. I waited to hear the only thing important to me: what she meant about "What has Simon Stucky done this time?"

On the radio an announcer said Kansas was having record temperatures for April. In other news, someone's dog had started acting weird, and it turned out the dog's animal instincts were telling him a hay bale was on fire. Somewhere a creek had flooded. "But we were lucky," a man's voice said. "Only one house with serious structural damage."

Lucky. Unless it was your house.

I saw a sign: LAVENDER FIELDS FOREVER. Great-aunt Dorcas turned in. The driveway curved around, toward rows of green plants leaning into a steep hill, then a red barn with tall cylinders behind it. Gravel crunched like granola under our wheels, and the car stopped.

I hopped out.

We were in the middle of nowhere. I saw fences and trees and lumpy hills as if a giant dog had flopped down and rolled around, flinging dirt and stones with its back paws. I looked at the old house. A ramp stuck out to one side. I followed Great-aunt Dorcas up crumbly cement steps between green bushes covered with white starfish flowers.

Had Dad run up these steps when he was my age? Had Grandma?

In the living room a ceiling fan whirred with a soft, creaking noise, and a white-haired elfish woman in a wheelchair snored softly.

"Micah asked after you." Great-aunt Dorcas raised her voice. "I brought Anna back to help with the pies."

This must be Great-aunt Lydia.

Great-aunt Dorcas kept talking, even though the elf woman was asleep. "You'd better change your mind and plan to come to the potluck."

The elf woman's eyes fluttered under her lids.

Great-aunt Dorcas marched me into the kitchen and proceeded to have no mercy on me. She sent me into the ooky-spooky musty-dusty basement for apples, and when I came dashing back up with a big shudder, she said, "The Lord loves a cheerful giver."

I almost mentioned that in case she hadn't heard, Abraham Lincoln had freed the slaves.

She opened the ancient refrigerator. "Mercy!" she said. "I don't have the eggs I thought I did."

Saved! I'd get to see the Oakwood grocery store.

"The chicken house is right close by, Anna." Great-aunt Dorcas walked over and opened the front door. "Take an empty carton from that shelf."

What?

She must have seen the horror on my face because she said, "You can't get lost. The paved path starts at the white eye-zalias. Head for the trees. Holler for Morgan, and she'll help you."

"I can't holler to someone I don't know," I politely explained.

"Mercy, Anna. Everyone around here is related to you." She waved at the corner. "Take Lydia. She'll be happy to keep you company."

How much company could a sleeping person be?

Luckily, I'd helped with wheelchairs plenty of times in church, so I walked bravely up to the elf woman. I set the egg carton in her sleeping lap.

Great-aunt Dorcas held the door open. "I promised the Good Lord as long as he gives me the strength, I would give every aid and comfort to Lydia." She sighed loudly. "Lydia, this is Anna. Micah's girl. Remember?"

I released the brake and eased the wheelchair across the room and over the door bump. I started down the ramp. The door banged softly shut behind us.

The elf person turned. Her face was as wrinkled as carrot roots. "And you know what the Lord loves." She winked. "A cheerful giver."

CHAPTER 13

⟳

TJ, Bob-Silver, Morgan, and the Monkey

Someone who was easy to startle might have let go of the wheelchair. When I got safely to level ground, Great-aunt Lydia said, "You come around and hug me like you mean it."

I wasn't used to hugging pure strangers. Her eyes looked up at me, blue-gray like Dad's. "Little Katherine's granddaughter," she said.

What burst out of my mouth was "How old are you?"

"Eighty-one." She gave a snort of laughter. "How did I get so soon old and so late smart?" She reached into her pocket, handed me a lemon drop, said something, and translated it: sweets for a sweet mouth.

"What's that language?" I asked.

"You don't recognize German?" She clicked her tongue. "*Ach, jammer.* My parents went to German school and English school." The rooty wrinkles deepened. "All of that is gone now."

I looked at her. "Were you really sleeping?"

"To everything there is a season," she said. "A time to talk and a time to keep silent."

As I pushed the wheelchair down the path, it was a time to talk. "I live still in the house where I was born," she told me.

"Is that where my grandma was born, too?"

"Mama said she would have her last two babies in the hospital." A chicken ran in front of us, and she clicked at it fiercely. "The rascal *will* keep escaping. Where's Morgan with that dog?"

"Who's Morgan exactly?" I asked. "What dog?"

"The dog that loves the chickens."

I imagined a dog writing chicken valentines.

The day was bright and hot and full of buzzings and whirrings on either side of us and then a faint boom-boom in the distance, so I aimed at the trees and stuck to the middle of the path. To our left was the big barn. "Are there horses?" I asked. "Can I ride them?"

Great-aunt Lydia shook her head. "*Ach*, it's all empty. But I used to take Little Katherine to see the horses. She helped me snip my braids by the light of the moon to make them grow faster. I taught her to make bread."

"I've never made bread," I said.

Great-aunt Lydia clicked as if I were a naughty chicken. "My mother said in Russia a girl could make bread before she could walk."

"Are we Russian?"

"*Ach, jammer,* no." She shook her head. "Swiss-German from Russia."

We were in tree shade now. I wiped sweat out of my eyes, and a giant slug landed on the back of my leg. I whirled around.

Oh. It wasn't a slug. A big silent dog had flupped

the back of my leg with its cool, wet nose. Another bounced toward us through the trees and sloppily smelled me up. "TJ!" Great-aunt Lydia said. "That's terrible rude. Poor TJ had to leave his work." She said something in German and translated. "Work makes the living sweet."

"What does a dog do for work?"

"He found people. Didn't you, TJ? Caroline says her dogs have the gift of nose, but now they're farmers."

Cousin Caroline was the cop who was going to fail at farming.

Something zoomed over our heads. I ducked. The dogs barked wildly. A girl's voice floated down. "TJ and Bob-Silver! Cease and desist."

I peered up through scraggle branches. A tree house. I felt itchy to get up there.

"Morgan?" Great-aunt Lydia called. "Is it you? What kind of pestilence are you sending down upon our heads?"

"A screaming monkey," a girl's voice said. "They sell them at the lumberyard. That's funny, isn't it?"

Wouldn't it be great if Morgan, whoever she was, said, "Come on up"?

Bob-Silver rustled through the grass and brought us a small stuffed monkey with a cape. "Is it for helping with the lavender?" Great-aunt Lydia called.

"It's not useful for anything," the voice called back. "I like it because I thought a lumberyard would only have lumber."

"Hurry you down and meet your third cousin." Great-aunt Lydia reached back to pat my hand. "Or are you Morgan's second cousin once removed?"

"I can't," Morgan called. "I'm working on my kings and queens project." Another monkey whistled through the air. I studied the tree house with longing.

"Caroline had an old farmhouse moved onto the property," Great-aunt Lydia said happily. "She makes terrible good pie; Dorcas has the sin of envy." She held up the egg carton, and we started off, the dogs huffing around us. By now I didn't really need a paved path to guide me.

I could follow the smell.

CHAPTER 14

ᖇᖇ

Angel of Death

I followed the smell out of the trees and saw a chicken house and a fenced chicken yard and a tall woman with a black braid. A clump of silver hair hung over her forehead. She was wearing a shirt that wouldn't rip even if she had lifted things and slung them around.

"Brave Caroline," Great-aunt Lydia said. "To farm these rocky old acres."

The dogs bounced over to Cousin Caroline. "So Mikey really did it." She walked up and shook my hand. "Welcome to Lavender Fields Forever."

She ran this farm all by herself? I looked at her with pure admiration.

A woman stooped through the door of the chicken house. She was wearing a baseball cap and had a sunshiny face. I predicted she might be another great-aunt, and as soon as she came up and introduced herself as Great-aunt Ruth, I knew I was right.

"Oh, happy day." She hugged me. "You tell your folks I'll wait for the potluck to say hello because I'm sure they've had quite enough family for now. Are you coming to the potluck then?" she asked Great-aunt Lydia, but she didn't wait for the answer. "I live in town, but I'm out to the farm every day to buy eggs. Best eggs in the world."

"That's because we have happy hens," Cousin Caroline said. "They don't need coffee to get going in the morning. They get busy catching as many bugs as they can, even though nobody gives them a medal for their personal best."

"Bob-Silver likes them," Great-aunt Ruth said. "Look at how he's pointing."

"Dogs retire, but they can't ignore their noses." Cousin Caroline smiled at me.

"You folks will become egg customers, too, I'll bet." Great-aunt Ruth tapped my head. "You ever need a ride, give me a jingle." She climbed into a blue pickup truck that had a big dent in its side and roared off, waving out the window.

"Morgan!" Cousin Caroline called. "Come meet Anna." She took the empty carton from Great-aunt Lydia. "Now that she's in fifth grade, that girl likes doing her lessons and projects in the tree house. Takes a bit to dig her out."

Homeschooled? Lucky duck. "How come you became a farmer?" I asked. "Dad said his mom used to say—" Oops. I stopped more words from flapping out.

Cousin Caroline smiled. "For a long time your grandma was my hero. She sang like an angel. One day she went to the city and bought a guitar, which was the boldest thing anyone I knew had done." She bent to yank a skinny root out of the ground.

"Dad plays the guitar," I said.

"I'm not surprised."

"Was it hard to become a farmer?" I asked.

Cousin Caroline unhooked the fence to the chicken yard. "First time I ordered a box of chicks, I could hear their shrill little peeps even with the post office doors closed." She continued into the chicken house, but her voice kept calling the story to us. "They always got quiet when Morgan and I picked them up, long as we supported their feet. Maybe it's how they know they're not being carried off by a cat."

I leaned on the wheelchair and waited. Cousin Caroline came back out. "Then a cold spell hit. A single chick survived. One day it was sturdy and running around. The next day I saw Angel, the mouser, with two yellow twig feet hanging out of her mouth. She slurped the feet in, crunched, and sat back to clean her whiskers."

Ugh. "So the chicks *all* died?"

"God's eye is on the sparrow," Great-aunt Lydia said fiercely. "Ha."

"I don't know if you can blame God." Cousin

Caroline reached over as if she would rub Great-aunt Lydia's ears but patted her instead. "Blame me for not knowing how to farm. Blame Angel, the cat, the angel of chick death. Next time we knew to put the chicks in a warm space we could close off completely."

She handed me the carton, heavy and warm. What was it like to hold a fresh egg? "Do you miss being a cop?" I asked.

"When I was in the city, my bones missed the land." Cousin Caroline looked at me with her gray eyes. "What about your father? I remember him as a wretched kid who chased me through the cornfields and tried to scare me with a frog."

"Did he scare you?"

She smiled. "I liked frogs. Still do." She looked around. "Come on. Morgan can catch up."

On the way back I heard that odd boom-boom in the distance and something beside the path rattled, making me jump.

"Seedpod." Was Cousin Caroline trying not to laugh?

"Oh." My face burned. "I thought maybe it was a rattlesnake."

"A snake doesn't want to meet you any more than you want to meet it. Just avoid tall brush and any deep, dark crevices."

"Do you hear that buzzing?" I stopped. "And"—I pointed—"see that smoke?"

"The buzzing is cicadas. They're early this year— noisy bugs, aren't they? The smoke is some farmer burning weeds."

I wanted to know if cicadas bit people, but I didn't want to seem babyish.

"I'd rather meet a snake than have a fire," Great-aunt Lydia said.

Uh-huh. "Me, too."

Cousin Caroline squeezed my shoulder. "I heard about those fires in Colorado. Aunt Lydia, give this girl a box of baking soda. Always a good thing to have around in case of fire."

Cousin Caroline was a one-person Safety Club.

She leaned over and kissed Great-aunt Lydia.

"I know I won't see you at the potluck, Auntie," she said, "but I'll see you there, Anna."

When we got back in the house, I parked the wheelchair and joined Great-aunt Dorcas at the scratched kitchen table. "Is that pie dough?" I asked. "Can I help?"

"I'll do the rolling. Can't serve up a Stucky pie with a crust as tough as pig hide." She glanced at Great-aunt Lydia and muttered, "No rest for the wicked."

We worked to the sound of apple curls dropping *plink-plink* into the compost bucket and the thump of the rolling pin. I helped Great-aunt Dorcas until we had a line of pies on the counter with pretty pinched crusts and apple juices bubbling. I hoped she would offer me a slice, but she didn't.

I hoped Morgan would come running up the ramp, but she didn't.

I hoped for a box of baking soda, and when Great-aunt Dorcas went in the other room, Great-aunt Lydia showed me one on the kitchen shelves I could have.

As Great-aunt Dorcas drove me away from

Lavender Fields Forever, I thought about angel grandma who had once been Little Katherine. Somewhere right around here she had looked up to see a pencil line tornado dropping down out of the sky.

That's when I heard the call: "Save your sister! Save the cat!"

CHAPTER 15
✎

Save Your Sister,
Save the Cat

<u>Safety Tips for Floods</u>

1. Do not stay in a flooded car.

2. If your car is swept underwater, DON'T PANIC. Stay calm and wait for it to fill with water, and then the doors will open.

3. Hold your breath and swim to the surface.

4. If you are swept into fast-moving floodwater, point your feet downstream.

5. Always go over obstacles. Never try to go under them.

ຄ ຄ ຄ

I looked at Great-aunt Dorcas, but she had her mouth firmly shut. Had I really heard something?

We drove back the way we had come. Were Isabella and Midnight H. Cat in bad danger? Maybe. After all, I'd been attacked. "What did Simon do before?" I asked. "You said, 'What has Simon Stucky done this time?'"

Great-aunt Dorcas looked severe. "He who goes about as a talebearer reveals secrets, but he who is trustworthy conceals a matter. Proverbs 11:13."

I didn't think it was being a talebearer to clear up a mystery, but I could see I wasn't going to change her mind. When she pulled into the driveway, I politely said good-bye and ran upstairs to put my baking soda with my *Safety Tips* booklet in the pink room. I looked in the mirror.

I hadn't turned into Moses either. "Save your sister! Save the cat!" Was God really talking to me? It wasn't an outloud voice, but it didn't seem exactly like any thought I'd had before.

Why me?

"Anna," I could almost hear Jericho saying, "you

are a child of God. Why not you?"

But how could I save Isabella and my cat? They were too small to run away from prairie fires or wolves or tornadoes— Who was I kidding? I was too small, too.

I picked up the *Safety Tips* booklet and paged through it. I could be prepared. I could watch out for any dangers—creeks that could flood, for example, or bales of hay on fire.

But how could I keep them in sight all the time? I had to go to school.

Or did I?

Midnight was sitting on the windowsill in the pink room. When I went over, her ears flicked forward. Did she smell dog on me? I stroked her twitchy back, wondering if she was planning an incredible journey home. "Don't give up yet," I whispered to her.

Mom poked her head in. "Isabella is down for her nap, and I saved lunch for you." She came in and put her arm around me. "So you got to see the farm?" She didn't wait for an answer before she walked me out to the stairs. "I . . . well . . . I know everyone here means to be kind."

Not everyone, I thought. *Not Simon.* I looked at her and saw the face of someone who was feeling bad— bad for letting Great-aunt Dorcas take me off and probably for not knowing much about casseroles and pies.

Poor Mom.

Mom let me eat beside her while she put books in a bookcase. I watched her bite her lip. I could tell she was already missing teaching history. "Can I help you with alphabetical order? I'm done." I showed her my fingers. "See?"

"Sure." She smiled and handed me a stack. *An. Ar. Be.* After a few minutes, I said, "Next time you teach about the gold rush, I predict you'll be telling your students you know why the forty-niners rushed right over Kansas, huh?"

Mom laughed. I hoped she would say, "This experiment is not quite what I thought it would be." Instead, she gave me one of her beloved history lessons. "Congress squabbled a long time about whether to let Kansas be a state. While they argued, floods left many families without a crop of any kind. Then the weather turned dry." She wiped a book with a rag. "When news came that Kansas finally was going to become a state, people whooped and hollered and fired Old Kickapoo cannon in the air."

"Tell me another Kansas disaster story," I said.

"Eighteen seventy-four." She gave a fake shiver, and I knew it was going to be juicy. "Rocky Mountain locusts plague. Twelve-point-five trillion locusts swarmed down in a mass bigger than California and ate all the crops."

I handed her books back. "I thought locusts died out after the plague Moses brought down on the Egyptians."

"Mo-om." Isabella's voice interrupted, wailing from upstairs.

Mom got up slowly. "For years, when the settlers plowed, they brought up shovelfuls of locust eggs. They're extinct now."

"Is Dad around?" I asked.

Mom pointed to the front door. I found him on the porch, looking into the afternoon heat shimmers. "Watch, Dad." I ran to the tree and pulled myself up. He gave me a thumbs-up that meant "some muscles." I dropped back down and nestled in beside him. Dad ran his knuckle down my hair part. "So you got to see the farm," he said. "Or what's left of it."

"Cousin Caroline said you chased her with frogs."

He laughed his good old rhinoceros laugh. "Did you see the pond?"

"I saw a barn," I told him. "I saw a chicken house."

The warmth was pressing on our heads. In Colorado we sometimes got *snow* this time of year. "Why won't Great-aunt Lydia come to the potluck?" I asked.

"Won't she?" He shook his head. "Long ago church people in Oakwood took sides over whether it was ever right to go to war. One night the church burned. Lydia was born not long after that. It was a hard story to grow up hearing, I think."

I squeezed his arm. "Dad, I think I should help Mom with Isabella tomorrow. Also, I need to tell you—"

Dad's pocket buzzed. To my surprise, he took his phone out and started listening. That was just wrong. Dad always said, "We rule our phones; our phones don't rule us." In Colorado he refused to interrupt real conversations for phone conversations. "Gandhi wouldn't be listening to his phone right now," I wanted to say.

Dad stood up. "The best way you can help is to go to school tomorrow. And sleep in your bed tonight. I need to get back to the church." He started off.

What? This was not the way my dad behaved.

"Morgan doesn't have to go to school," I shouted after him.

I watched the soles of his feet disappear. When I was little, I would stand on Dad's shoes and dance around his office. Even now, when Jericho and I visited, I did it when we were feeling silly.

But in Kansas, I reminded myself, Dad had to fix

a hump. That meant he *had* to be very serious and maybe even let his phone rule him.

Inside, I made a living room corner playground for Midnight H. Cat. Then Mom and Isabella and I worked on preparing the basement. One warm jacket apiece. Rubber-soled shoes. The fireproof lockbox with important documents.

In the late afternoon Dad called Mom to say he wasn't coming home for supper. Appalling! He hadn't even come home by bedtime. Mom didn't say anything when I put the sleeping bag in the hall, so I curled up there with Midnight H. Cat, praying without ceasing that God would remind Dad about having an understanding heart.

CHAPTER 16

✿

Meeting Morgan

The second morning in Oakwood, Kansas, I woke up in the pink room again. A note was beside me on the pillow. "We know changes aren't easy. Take one more day home from school. Love, Dad."

Maybe it was an answer to prayer.

At breakfast Midnight H. Cat purred in my lap while I ate. Mom said, "This would be a good day to try taking your cat outside."

I shook my head. "I don't think so."

It was a miracle I even had my cat. Luckily, my teacher this year was a big fan of democracy, and our class voted to try to walk instead of having our parents drive us to school. That's why Mom and Isabella and I heard noises of desperation coming from a roof. I went tearing back to my house to get Dad. He climbed up the fire escape and reached down the chimney and hauled out a shivering, clawing black kitten.

By then a bunch of fourth graders were standing around. Half voted to name the cat Midnight, and half voted for Halloween. A perfect tie. Peacemaker Dad wrote "Midnight H. Cat" on the form at the vet's office. Why did we save her, though, if we were going to move her to Kansas and freak her out?

I set her on the floor, got up, and studied the backyard. It had a shed. What if she crawled under and a skunk was waiting there? What if the mean kid, Simon, was lurking around? "By the way," I said, "I need a flashlight and fire extinguisher."

Upstairs, Isabella hollered, "Mom!"

Mom sighed. "I'll call your dad and tell him you're coming over to discuss safety supplies."

What Mom had asked for was three hours a day of

writing time. So far what she was getting was zero hours.

When I got to the church, Dad was outside studying the church sign. "I bet you're wondering what to put next," I said as I ran up.

He laughed. "There ain't no flies on Anna. Got any good ideas?"

He tipped his head to one side, studying the sign, then hooked my arm and sang, "Oh, give me a home where the buffalo roam." He grinned at me. "Kansas state song."

Dad had gone from the Beach Boys to buffaloes.

"You know what I need?" I said. "A flashlight. Also, I wanted to tell you—"

"Hey, hey," Dad said, "what's this?"

Across the parking lot came Cousin Caroline pushing Great-aunt Lydia in her wheelchair with a violin in her lap. The person behind them carrying a basket must be Morgan—tall and bold like her mom.

"Bet you didn't know that one of your ancestors arrived in America with nothing but a hat and a violin," Dad told me.

"Of course I didn't. You never told me anything about your roots."

"I'm sorry." He sounded sorry. "Did I tell you about our ancestor who could catch flies with his bare hands?"

I guess there weren't no flies on him. How many kids in school already knew that story?

The family parade was close now, and Great-aunt Lydia pointed her violin bow at Dad. "What did you mean by staying away for so long?"

"What do you mean by going cantankerous?" He leaned over and kissed her. I was having a hard time breathing, with feelings taking up all the air. After a minute Dad said, "The last time I visited . . . well . . . I'm sure my mother never meant to upset everyone so much."

"*Ach.*" Great-aunt Lydia clicked her tongue. "You come out to the farm on Monday. I'll make lunch. Remember *mak kuchen*?" She took his hand as if he were a kid.

Morgan headed toward a garden bed at the side of the church lawn, and even though we hadn't been officially introduced, I followed, trying to see inside the basket, as if I were two giant eyeballs on legs.

She pulled a seed packet out.

"Did you know it's not true that moss only grows on the north side of trees?" I asked. "If you get lost, remember that a forest thick enough to get lost in is thick enough for moss to grow anywhere."

"Really?" she said. At least she wasn't a *sixth* grader, all full of her own awesomeness. Maybe I could even show her my disaster notebook.

"By the way," I said, "great tree house." She gave me a fifth-grader-I-come-in-peace face, so I went on. "At least what I could see looked interesting. There's not that much interesting around here, so—" Oops. That might be insulting. "I guess you've been learning a lot about farming."

"Uh-huh." She held up the packet. "Bean seeds."

"You can see Pikes Peak from my house," I said. "Unless it's cloudy. You moved here two years ago, right? Wasn't it hard to leave the city? Is it always this hot here?"

Morgan put the packet down. "Come on. I'll show you something interesting."

I left Dad talking to Great-aunt Lydia and followed Morgan around to the back of the church. "Have you personally seen a tornado?" I asked. "Because my grandma did. Almost anyway."

"And they left the baby upstairs," Morgan said. "I hear that story every family reunion."

Hey. I wasn't used to someone else having *my* personal family stories. I was staring up at a stained glass angel with spread wings, and I almost tripped over a curved flat stone.

Apparently the something interesting Morgan wanted to show me was a graveyard.

CHAPTER 17

⌒⌒

The Children's Graves

We were behind the church, and the stained glass angel was staring from high above. There were rows of gravestones with grass and dandelions in between. I also saw a few benches and pots of red geraniums.

"That's where my grandma's buried." Morgan pointed. "Your grandma was supposed to be buried beside her."

My grandma was buried in California. "People don't just stay in the ground, you know," I said. "They become angels and stuff like that. Are there hundreds of generations of our ancestors here?"

"Not hundreds," Morgan said. "Our great-grandpas were born in Russia. Keep coming." I followed gingerly through the gravestones, trying not to step on anyone's bones. "Ta-da." Morgan pointed to three small, old stones.

I bent over and read: "Charity." Nobody would name a kid that, would they? It was probably an adult. An old woman who was all withered up and happy to die.

I touched the name on the second stone. "Faith," it said. And the name on the third one was "Hope." I knelt on the prickly grass.

All three stones had the same dates: 1878–1888.

This was not savory. Not savory at all.

Morgan plopped on a bench that had "And I shall dwell in the house of the Lord forever" carved on the back. "It was the children's blizzard," she said.

I rubbed Faith's name softly. The stone was rough, and my stomach felt like it was curling around the edges like spiders do when they die. Where were the sirens? Didn't Oakwood at least have a bell in 1888?

"The prairies were unusually warm that day,"

Morgan said in a storyteller way. "Men went off to farms and children went to school with light coats or no coats at all."

The questions didn't make sense, but my brain kept asking them anyway. Where were the fire trucks and ambulances? Where was 911? "This is a gruesome story," I said, "isn't it?"

"It's okay if you can't handle it," Morgan said.

"Okay," I said. "Go on." I joined her on the bench and leaned my head against the word *forever*.

"Here's what happened," Morgan said. "A gray cloud loomed in the sky. Faith, Hope, and Charity were in a one-room school."

"Have mercy," I wanted to say. Instead, I said, "Didn't they have a safety plan?"

Morgan said the three girls left the school holding on to a rope so they wouldn't lose one another. "But within minutes a wall of ice crystals and hurricane winds slammed into everything. The winds threw snow high into the air, blinding and suffocating man and beast."

I focused on one feather in the stained glass angel's left wing. Violin music floated around from the front of the church. Great-aunt Lydia must be playing for Dad. My eyelids wouldn't stop blinking. What about angels? Where were the angels?

"All over the prairies, people were scrambling for shelter," Morgan said. "No one had a chance to get a rescue party together or anything like that."

Did kids' brains at least go numb if they got that cold?

Did Faith, Hope, and Charity wish, wish, wish they'd done something different? "I guess they died, huh?" That was obvious. The gravestones.

"Our great-grandpa was in that blizzard, too." Morgan gave me a nod to say, *another story we have to share.* "He said the snow came as if it had slid out of a sack."

Shiverydee. The angel in the window was holding something that might be a shepherd's staff, but maybe it was something to whack the evil and the insincere with.

Morgan leaned close. I felt her breath puff on my sweaty neck. "He said it was as dark as a root cellar. You could hold up your hand, but you couldn't see it."

"I guess he survived," I said, "or we wouldn't be here."

"He almost lost his feet. They were frozen solid, but his friend said, 'Put them under my coat and right here against my heart.'"

Morgan was a great storyteller. I sat on the bench listening to her go on, with my legs swinging back and forth, looking up at the angel and feeling massively glad that by the time of the next Kansas blizzard we'd be far, far away.

CHAPTER 18

❧

Preparation Is
Better than Hope

When Cousin Caroline called to Morgan that it was time to finish planting the beans, we went back to the front of the church. I told Dad about the safety supplies, and he found a flashlight in his office desk. "Come on," he said. "I'll walk you home."

As we crossed the parking lot, I said, "By the way, *nobody* in Grandma's family is old and weak. Did you know Great-aunt Lydia is eighty-one?"

He nodded. "Aunt Lydia said their eighty-year-old brother—your great-uncle—went skydiving last month." His phone rang.

"Doesn't the church have a secretary?" I asked.

"Nope." He tapped my head. "But that call can wait until after lunch."

We were at the field now. I wondered if seeing an angel here was a onetime thing. "Do you think angels still bring messages to people?" I asked.

"Angels." Dad rubbed his chin. "They're pretty complicated."

At lunch I launched right into telling Morgan's story. By the time I got to "Great-grandpa and his friend tried to find their house," Mom was looking pale. Morgan's words were bright in my brain. "Ice hung from their whiskers and almost suffocated their faces, but they staggered on. They shouted, but no echoing voice returned."

Mom frowned. "I'm not sure this is appropriate for Isabella."

"Don't worry," I said. "Dad wouldn't have been born if it had a sad ending."

"That's a relief," Dad said.

I ignored him. "They thought they'd have to kneel

down and die, but finally they saw a hog shed. More dead than alive, they crowded in among the hogs."

Mom was still frowning.

"Happy ending now," I said quickly. "Great-grandpa's feet got saved by his friend. And the friend put *his* feet under a hog."

Dad tweaked Isabella's nose. "Never give up hope."

Preparation was better than hope. Pompeii, for example. Some people sat around, hoping ash wouldn't bury them, when they should have been rowing into the ocean as fast as they could go.

I imagined the one-room schoolhouse teacher opening the door to swirling snow. Telling Faith, Hope, and Charity, "Stay together and don't lose one another." I wouldn't say that part in front of Isabella. Too massively sad. Instead, I said, "Good thing we'll be out of Kansas soon, huh?"

All the rest of that day people rang the doorbell and brought more casseroles and potatoes. Every time I made sure Midnight H. Cat didn't slip out. When someone brought us some cans of corn, I took them to the basement. "Are we poor now?" I asked Mom when I got back up. "Do you even know things to make with all these potatoes?"

Mom laughed. "No," she said. "And yes. Or at least I can try."

"I'll bet you miss your Friday yoga class," I said. "Do you think you'll forget how to do your yoga poses if we don't get back to Colorado right away?"

"Yes," Mom said. "And no, I won't forget."

That night, before I took the sleeping bag to the hall, thunder boomed and smashed. I read *Kansas Safety Tips* by the night-light and then opened my Safety Notebook.

Tornado? Check.

Fire? I had baking soda so far.

Locusts? Extinct.

Wolves and feral hogs wouldn't come into town, I was pretty sure. But I should help Isabella practice wildlife safety just in case.

CHAPTER 19

The Power of Jell-O

The third day in Oakwood was Saturday, and I woke up in my sleeping bag in the hall for the first time. Victory! Small . . . but a victory.

Now to find out more about a kid who would throw a water balloon at me. Before I got downstairs, Dad gave me a squeeze. "Off to the lumberyard and grocery store. Gotta get some beans for bean soup."

Dad and his bean soup. He loved to cook it no matter what else we had in the house. "It's not my favorite," I reminded him.

He grinned. "Luckily, starvation doesn't set in for days."

I ran after him onto the porch. "Get a fire extinguisher, okay? And check to see if they have any screaming monkeys."

He waved. I climbed my tree onto the branch and sat on it, smelling the steamy air. A man walked by pushing a lawn mower—just like a weekend back in Colorado. Then I heard a squeaking sound.

Uh-oh. I got ready to duck.

But it was just a teenage girl holding the hand of a little girl trying to balance on in-line skates. "Hey," I called.

"What are you doing?" the little girl called back.

They came closer. "Are you the people who moved into the church house this week?" the teenager asked.

Well, I was *one* of the people. They looked like their family might have come from Mexico, not Russia. "You aren't my cousins, are you?" I asked.

The teenager shook her head. "I'm Mae. My sister is Slurpee."

"Slurpee?"

"That's my *nickname*. Watch." The little girl tipped up on her skates. Good thing she wasn't related to me or she could have been Slurpee Stucky.

"I'm Anna." I swung down. "Do you by any chance know where my cousin Simon lives?" I had lots more questions, but first things first.

"We know Simon." Slurpee looked at her sister. Mae nodded. "Want to see his house?"

I tore inside to tell Mom. She let me take a hard-boiled egg and juice box, and she walked me to the door to meet Mae. "I'll be right back," I called to Isabella.

Mae led us over a small bridge. "That's North Emma Creek," she said.

"Hi, North Emma Creek," Slurpee said. She waved at the water.

It was like we were wading into Oakwood. My brain wanted it to be like my Colorado neighborhood, with a coffee shop and college dorms and a giant, crooked sculpture chair outside an art museum. When Jericho and I came to the crosswalks, Jericho would always shout, "Mountains! Right there! See?"

But Oakwood was flat and square, with some fluffy white trees like fancy, show-off princesses standing in the middle of someone's plain old kitchen. A woman kneeling by a garden called, "Stay cool!" No kids (except for Slurpee). They must be inside their houses, doing whatever Kansas kids thought was fun or funny.

"School's down that block." Mae pointed to the left. "See the roof?" Then the sidewalk sloped a bit, and Slurpee started rolling faster, and Mae and I had to trot. "Here." Mae pointed. "That's where Simon and his grandma live."

The house had a fence around it and curved windows and stone lion heads with tongues dangling down. Beautiful. But strange.

I leaned my forehead on the fence. A grandma? What about his parents? Is that why Simon was mean? My hair felt frizzy, and so did my thoughts. "They have a lot of pink trees in their yard," I said.

"Redbuds," Mae said confidently. "Some people eat the flowers."

If Simon and his grandma had munched any redbud flowers, the trees had grown more flowers seriously fast.

"I need—" Slurpee pulled her sister down and whispered in her ear.

"Oops," Mae said. "Gotta run. Can you find your way back?"

"Sure."

They rushed off with Slurpee waving one arm in circles to keep her balance. I studied the house, ready to duck if someone came out, wondering what the deal was with Simon.

Finally I ran home and rang our doorbell for fun. When Mom opened the door, I saw a whiskery face by her feet. "Don't let the cat out!" I shouted.

"Anna, you can't keep her a prisoner inside forever." Mom scooped Midnight H. Cat up. Isabella crawled out between Mom's legs.

"We aren't going to be here *forever.*" My fingernails dug into my palms.

"But you want her to be happy no matter how long or short we're here."

I could feel worry wrinkling up my face. "At least let me get her favorite toy. And will you help make sure she doesn't run away?"

After I got the green jingly mouse, I guided Mom down the porch steps and showed her how to put Midnight H. Cat on the tree branch beside her green mouse. If my cat leaped down and dashed off, would I have the strength of a hundred people like in stories?

Mom stepped back. I held out my arms, tense as a rubber band. "Get ready to help me catch her if she heads to the backyard," I told Mom and Isabella. "If she gets under that shed in the back, she could get trapped or something."

Midnight sharpened her claws in the bark, perfectly calm. "See?" Mom gave a little whistle. "Want me to help you up, too?"

"I can do it." I pulled myself up and hung on the branch all limp with relief in the humid air. "What are you taking to the potluck?" I asked Mom.

"The salad with jicama and bell peppers and lime juice and cilantro." Mom looked proud. "I brought the ingredients all the way in the cooler."

If Mom didn't usually skip the potlucks at our Colorado church, she would know the three best ingredients.

Jell-O.
Pineapple chunks.
Marshmallows.

But I wasn't about to reveal the secret power of Jell-O. The faster this experiment was over, the better.

CHAPTER 20

ᘐ

Forget, Forgive, and Forget

That first Sunday morning in Kansas, I woke up wanting to help Dad get off on the right foot. I really did! But Isabella was clingy, and no matter how Mom and I tried, we couldn't get to the church on time. Inside, Mom showed me an arrow pointing upstairs to the fourth- and fifth-grade Sunday School class. "Think you can handle getting there by yourself?"

I nodded, although I felt like Daniel heading into the lions' den.

Step, step. Loud on the stairs. Did Daniel go all draggy shoes? Step. Step. I never felt *new* in our

Colorado church because I first went there the week after I was born. Step. Step. The aspens by our Colorado church would have new leaves, now, like pale green coins. *Last step.* I peeked into a small room with a long table and luckily an empty chair beside Morgan. I slid into it. "You're the preacher's kid," a boy said.

Morgan flipped a pencil at him. "I think she might know that."

Everyone laughed. The teacher said, "Welcome. I'm Mrs. Miller." She went around the room to do official and polite introductions and then asked, "How many of you are related to Anna?"

Hands waved. "Could be worse," Morgan whispered. "Seven of the eight grandparents of the last Spanish Hapsburg king were descended from just two people."

"What?" I whispered back.

"Shh."

By now I'd forgotten most of the names, which made me feel sweaty and not because it was warm in this room.

Right away Mrs. Miller solved the mystery on the church sign by asking us what we thought the Bible meant by saying we should forgive seventy times seven.

"So if I don't know how to multiply, I don't have to forgive anyone?" a boy named Chad asked. Some kids laughed. Luckily, he was not related to me.

Mrs. Miller obviously thought it was better to ignore inappropriate comments. "When someone says *forgiveness,* what do you think?"

"Forgive and forget," a fifth grader named Kylee said.

Morgan said, "Some things people can't forget. Like if you're a queen and your father beheaded your mother, you aren't going to forgive him, and you sure aren't going to forget."

A boy whose name I'd forgotten raised his hand. "My grandma told Morgan's mom that old farm can't pay the bills and if she thinks it can, she doesn't have the sense God gave geese. Morgan's mom hasn't forgiven and forgotten my grandma."

Wow. I glanced at Morgan. A lions' den might

smell like blood and death, but lions didn't make personal remarks.

Chad jumped in. "What about Simon? My mom says he's only an eight-year-old, and people should forgive him." He waved toward me. "And what about when her grandma sold her acres and the family didn't forgive her?"

Personal remarks about *my very own grandmother.*

"And you can shut up," Morgan said.

Mrs. Miller looked a little desperate. "Those are all good questions. No one said forgiveness is easy. Who else has a thought?"

I sat in a strange room that smelled like baby powder wondering what Chad meant about Simon. Finally Mae said, "It's when someone does something bad to you and deserves something bad back, but you don't do it."

Luckily, a bell rang, and no one else had to talk about forgiveness. When we were going out the door, Chad asked Morgan. "Where *is* your dad really?"

Morgan gave him a look and clattered away down the stairs before I could pry.

In the sanctuary the sun lit up the sheep in the stained glass window and turned the plain glass windows to shining rectangles. During the announcements, Mom and Isabella and I stood up. I tried to smile normally, which is hard when you don't know where to make your eyes look. Slurpee—in the pew in front of us—blew me a kiss. I didn't see Simon. Or Morgan.

Dad started the sermon with a joke, and I laughed extra loud to be loyal. Then he said, "Thank you for inviting me to help in a time of change." He smiled. "We get the funny idea God wants us to always be comfortable. When we're uncomfortable, instead of sticking with it and eventually growing, we put all our energy into fighting whatever is making us uncomfortable."

I sneaked a look around. Were people listening?

Actually, maybe he was talking about me. That would be unfair because nobody should have to be comfortable in a pink room.

On the church wall was a banner with red flames

licking up it, which made my brain remember holding Dad's hand and looking at the ridge of mountains as planes flew over to drop fire retardant in trails of bright red. And that made me think about the day I kicked the same-sames out of the Safety Club.

Ever since I was in preschool, I'd had those same-same friends—Lilya and Tigerlily and Clare, same block, same church, same school. Of course I invited them to join the Safety Club. It was great for a while. Then Lilya complained about the rules. A week later Clare wasn't prepared when it was her turn to present.

The worst was the day I had researched forest fires. "If the fire gets too close and you know you can't escape," I was saying, "get in a ditch. Your feet should be facing toward the fire." I looked up and saw Lilya was giggling. "You're out!" I said.

"Don't we get a vote?" Clare asked.

"We all belong in this club, too," Lilya said.

"No." I said. "I made up this club and it's my house and you all belong out."

Jericho told me later, "Thinking of fire could have

made Lilya nervous, you know. Sometimes people behave in strange ways when they're nervous."

But I . . .

Oops. I suddenly realized Dad was finishing up and I hadn't been paying attention. "Difficult as it is," he was saying, "forgiveness sets us free. Not only so the person who has done wrong can have another chance. Also so we don't have to carry the weight of frustration and bitterness around."

Great-aunt Dorcas sucked in her breath. It was quick, but I heard it.

As we opened our hymnbooks, Slurpee's mom leaned over in the pew in front of us and whispered to Slurpee. "This song was written one hundred and fifty years ago. People have been going to church for two thousand years."

When it was time for the benediction, Dad raised his arms and said, "God invites us to the freshness of new beginnings."

Unluckily, there was probably zero chance for new beginnings in a church after 2000 years.

CHAPTER 21

∞

Bad Luck at the Potluck

<u>Safety Tips for Fires</u>

1. Check your smoke alarms every month to be sure the batteries work.

2. Make an escape plan, including where your family will meet outside. Practice it.

3. If you're in a fire, crawl. Smoke and heat rise.

4. Stop, drop, and roll—and keep your hand over your mouth.

5. Sprinkle baking soda, not water, on an electrical fire.

∞ ∞ ∞

After our Sunday casserole lunch, Dad headed right back to church to change the sign. "My new Kansas Sunday routine," he said.

In Colorado our Sunday routine was driving up into the mountains. Sometimes we hiked in wildflowers, all tiny and red or purple. Sometimes we saw deer with velvet ears. Sometimes Grandpa met us with surprises—a zip line or balloon or train ride. "What will your special message be?" I asked.

"Wait and see." He gave me a grin.

"Can you help me find the right place for the new fire extinguisher?" Mom asked me. "Right after I put Isabella down for her nap?"

Of course. "But wouldn't you rather write?"

"Oh, well." She took Isabella's hand. "Some change can be good."

Really? Because what we already had in Colorado was perfect. I didn't believe what she'd said, and I knew she actually didn't either.

That afternoon Dad came home one time, to load boxes of books into the car and drive them back to the church. Mom and I were putting the fire extinguisher right by the kitchen door because the directions in my Safety Notebook said to put it in the room where most fires happen, in plain sight and easy to reach.

"We need one for upstairs, too, right?" Mom asked. She was very smart and usually very helpful.

When Isabella woke up, she and I played hide-and-pounce with Midnight H. Cat while Mom made her salad. Then we practiced SMART in case we saw a wolf or feral hog.

1. Stop; do not run.
2. Make yourself look big.
3. Announce, "Leave me alone!"
4. Retreat; back away slowly.
5. Tell an adult.

On the walk to the church that evening, the air smelled green and warm. Mom had her arms wrapped around a big painted bowl, and she looked nervous.

I showed Isabella things: prickly brown pods like

tiny troll heads; a worm squiggling on the sidewalk. "Do worms have teeth?" Isabella asked.

I told her they didn't, but she grabbed Mom's leg anyway. At the corner I read the sign. BLESSED ARE THE PURE IN HEART. My heart was pretty pure, I thought.

I wanted to ask Mom if people were going to watch us actually eat. Because chewing can be pretty disgusting. Instead, I said, "I'll help Isabella down the stairs."

Step. Step. The basement smelled like ham. Adults and kids were covering tables with white paper. "Stay here," I told Isabella. I went over to the dessert table to check if my pies were there.

Not yet.

Behind me I heard a man say, "Hold on there, young lady."

I whirled around. Isabella was on a chair by the salad table. "But I like those hairy green things," she said.

Two kids putting forks on tables laughed. I hurried over to her. "Kiwi," I said. "Not hairy green things. And we have to wait."

Her face started to crumple. I managed to lift her—even though she was as heavy as a full dresser drawer—and stagger away. Isabella's head blocked my view, which is why I didn't know something was in front of me until it snagged my ankle.

I yelped. As I was going down, I caught one tiny glimpse of Simon. Then I fell flat on my sister.

Isabella let out a howl and grabbed my shirt. I rolled off—and heard a ripping sound. Shiverydee! I pinched her, because sometimes it's good to do something stupid so you won't do something even stupider. Suddenly Morgan's face was right there. "Help," I gasped out.

I managed to get Isabella's arms. Morgan grabbed her legs, hollering, "Ouch! Don't kick." We hustled Isabella up and out onto the lawn, where she kept screaming and her nose started bleeding and where Mom and Cousin Caroline found us.

"Help me get her home," Mom called over Isabella's screaming. As we hauled Isabella off, I saw Aunt Dorcas. Pinch mouthed.

No one tried to talk until we got onto the porch, and Morgan, who was the only one not hanging on to some part of Isabella, grabbed her nose. Isabella shut up. "Stinky worms." She let out a huge hiccup.

I looked at the slime streaking our door. She was right about the stinky. It wasn't worms, though. Someone knew where to find eggs that had been laid a long, long time ago and had sat around somewhere getting rotten.

I had a feeling I knew exactly who that someone was.

CHAPTER 22

Stinky Oakwood

Simon must have followed us to the church. While Isabella was having her fit, he had time to get back here.

Why did he have to be mean upon mean?

I ran upstairs to change my shirt and ran back downstairs. Caroline had been scarily fast at finding a bucket and a brush and was scrubbing the door. "Really?" Mom was saying to her. "That's pretty shocking."

"What's shocking?" I asked.

"Shh," Morgan said. I went over to sit beside her.

"True story," she whispered. "About when people would come home and find paint, not eggs, splashed on their houses."

Isabella had her head in Mom's lap. "Sorry," I mouthed to her.

"America was at war, and Germany *was* the enemy," Cousin Caroline said. "Here in Kansas our ancestors were refusing to pick up guns. They spoke German at home and church as if they might be German spies."

"Were they spies?" I muttered to Morgan.

She shook her head. "Peacemakers."

Cousin Caroline said people, including some of our ancestors, would find their houses painted yellow as a way to say, "You're a chickenhearted traitor and no-good neighbor of mine." She said something low. I heard the word *dynamite*.

"What got blown up?" I asked.

"I didn't hear Caroline say anything got blown up," Mom said. "Why don't you go back to the church and keep Dad company?"

Morgan and I took off running, and the whole way

I wondered if Simon's ancestors had thrown dynamite at mine. Or maybe mine had thrown dynamite at his.

We clattered into the church and down the basement steps. At the bottom Morgan turned around with her finger on her lips. Dad was standing by the long main dish table saying the blessing.

I peeked over Morgan's shoulder. About forty people were standing around with bowed heads. A woman with bluish halo hair. Sunday School kids. Slurpee looking all hungry face at the dessert table.

I bent close to Morgan's ear. "What's Simon's problem?" The s's came out in a hiss.

"Church," she whispered back.

"Why?" My voice came out louder than I'd planned.

"Amen." Dad opened his eyes and frowned in my direction.

Morgan slid toward a basement pillar, and I slid after her. A woman handed Dad a plate. "Start us off, Pastor. You're the guest of honor. And where's your family?"

Dad looked around, a bit desperately.

"Let's get in line," Morgan said. "I don't want my mom's pie to run out before I get dessert. We can talk about Simon later."

"*When?*" Oops. That was loud. Now a bunch of people were looking at us, even the people who were pretending they weren't.

Shiverydee.

I *really* didn't mean to get Dad off on any wrong feet. But I could tell I was going to be flat out no good at anything in this church.

CHAPTER 23

୬୦

Shiverydee

My number one job at the potluck was taking double helpings of Mom's salad to be loyal. My next job was to tell Dad about Simon, and now I had two more things he'd done, too. But there were church members who wanted Dad's attention just as much, and they had gotten to him first.

I glanced around. Morgan's table had filled up with other kids. I could crowd in and talk about the bear or something interesting. But some or all of them had seen me fall flat on my sister and get my shirt ripped. What a pathetic way to get started.

Instead, I slid onto the other end of Dad's bench and concentrated on eating, which wasn't easy because people kept coming over to say welcome and give Dad their opinions. "I hear Simon was in the basement earlier," a woman's voice said over my head. "He needs to stay away until he makes a public apology."

Great-aunt Ruth came over to hug Dad. "God put something noble and good into every heart," she murmured.

Behind me a man added, "And every child should be welcome in church."

"Old feelings," another man said. "Stirred up like so much pig feed."

Someone with a purple bracelet blocked my view. "It's a sad shame that our beloved minister decided it was time to retire. But thank goodness you're here."

Even Great-aunt Dorcas came over—to tell Dad it wasn't appropriate for Morgan to plant beans in the flower bed.

If I closed my eyes, my brain could almost think I was back in Colorado. The other same-sames and I used to sit together at potlucks. Here . . . I heard steps and looked up to see Cousin Caroline slip in. Alone.

I didn't get close to Dad until the dishes were stacked in the giant dishwasher and the tables were wiped and people had wrapped up the plates of leftovers. Then we started out into the warm evening, loaded with leftovers and Mom's painted bowl.

As we walked to the parking lot, I finally got to tell Dad all about Simon and the rotton eggs. "Why does he have to apologize to the church?" I asked.

"He threw a rock through the stained glass window." Dad put the plates of leftovers on the car hood and opened the back door. "Some people think we should make a very big deal about it. Others don't." He put the leftovers on the backseat. "Small towns can be like spiderwebs: if you touch one part, another part jangles."

"But what do *you* think?" I asked.

"Let me show you something." Dad opened the passenger door. "Hop in."

We drove out of Oakwood. The welcome sign was black against the sunset, and I felt small compared with the sky but also bigger and safer now that Dad was involved with solving Simon.

A few minutes later the car slowed down, eased into the grass, and stopped. I got out. The moon was a munched-down curved cookie. In the starry light, I could see that we were in the clearing with that wooden cowboy and horse. I followed Dad across ankle-prickling grass. Now I could see a wire cross filled with flowers, too. "What's that creaking noise?" I asked.

"Frogs."

I leaned against Dad, feeling his breath on the top of my head as he told me a terribly sad story about Simon, whose mom died when he was a baby. "This year Simon's dad was riding in a church motorcycle fundraiser," Dad said. "A storm blew up with thunder and lightning, and he pulled his motorcycle into this clearing to wait it out."

Dad's voice dissolved and quit. "Did the lightning hit him?" I peered at the wooden horse's eyes that peered back at me. "Did he die?"

Dad squeezed me. "Yes, Anna. He did."

I stood as still as Lot's salt wife in the hot, froggy evening, with the air smelling watery like the inside of a tin camping cup. "At the funeral," Dad said, "the minister said God had called Simon's father home. I guess he didn't think how that would sound to Simon. Simon ran out of church and threw that rock."

It was awful. Why should Simon take it out on me, though? "I've decided," I said, "I don't want to go to school. Not while Simon is there."

Dad took a crunchy step toward the car. "I've never seen it work to run away from problems. It's only four weeks until summer vacation."

He said that as if four weeks weren't a month—like the guy who comes on television and says, "All this for only one hundred forty-nine dollars and ninety-nine cents."

"Think about it," I wanted to say. What kinds of mean things had Simon already spread about me?

In Colorado Dad would have listened, but before I could open my mouth, he said, "I want you to get a good sleep tonight. In your bed."

When we got home, I sat in the stupid pink room. It felt like a bunch of sadness was stuck on me. Like flies.

I already knew—because of the wildfires—that it was impossible to stop every bad thing. My dad's changing. Simon's dad dying. Hope, Faith, and Charity. The blizzard froze eyelashes shut, Morgan said, and plugged noses. Ice masks hung on their faces. Too fierce for even the bravest of girls.

Tears came leaking out while Midnight H. Cat licked them off my chin.

The real way to keep us all safe was to get us back to our very own house in our very own city. Too bad my call contradicted Dad's call, but live by the sword, die by the sword.

CHAPTER 24

֍

Make Haste to Get Us Home

<u>Safety Tips for Peace Protests</u>

1. Don't come or go to a protest alone.

2. Don't wear jewelry that might get yanked or pulled.

3. Look friendly to remind police officers you are a human being and they are, too.

4. Sing. It's good for courage.

5. If necessary, assume the nonviolent position: head between your knees; elbows together in front of your eyes; hands over your head.

֍ ֍ ֍

The longer I sat in that pink room, the more determined I got. I was *not* going to go to school, the only new kid. With four weeks left, Simon could pop around any corner. A personal comment about my family could pop out anytime. And I had work to do to get us back to Colorado.

I started to pray. "Make haste," I said out loud. It sounded good and strong. "Make haste to save your people." I put my two hands on my heart. It really did feel stronger. When Jericho and I were taking one of our famous exploring walks around the city—or Grandpa and I were hiking—a stronger heart would come in handy.

I checked my Safety Notebook, got out a pencil and paper and wrote a note, and then crept down the hall to Mom and Dad's bedroom and peeked in. Mom was in the bed, already asleep. I went over and touched her rumpled short hair. "Let my people go," I whispered into her ear.

That's what Moses said. I thought about Moses in the Bible picture, all stern and commanding with his arm straight out.

Mom smiled faintly. Even sleeping people could take things into their brains.

I went back and carried my sleeping bag into the hall. I stretched out on it and wiggled to get it straight and smooth. I closed my eyes. Someone stepped right on me. "Ow," I said.

"Sorry." It was Isabella.

She creaked down the stairs. After a while I followed.

In the living room Dad was in a chair with his eyes closed with Isabella and my cat in his lap. I sat on the floor beside them. A paw landed softly on my head. "Midnight H. Cat," Dad said sleepily. "What a distinguished name."

"Can we put her name on our mailbox when we go back to Colorado?"

"Maybe. When the cat runs for Congress."

Midnight yawned. "She likes you," I said.

"Sure. When I snore, she thinks I'm purring."

"Did you know God lives in our stomachs?" Isabella asked drowsily.

I held in a giggle. Anyway, why not? It was like Dad had always had a different Micah Nickel living in his stomach, one that only thought about a church and didn't play the guitar.

"Dad?" I nudged his arm and held up my note for him to read: *Remember Martin Luther King and Gandhi?* "Sleeping in the hall is my silent protest," I said. "Fighting injustice the peacemaker's way. Like you've talked about."

Dad sighed. "All right, Anna."

"Also," I said, "I should definitely come to the farm with all of you tomorrow."

His breath huffed out heavily. "One more day out of school then."

"Do you want me to take Isabella to bed?" I asked. "I'm strong enough to carry her on my back."

Dad lifted her toward me. I poked her soft middle. She yawned. "You just poked God."

All the way up the stairs I could feel change creaking in the air. The first thing I'd do when I got back to Colorado was buy goody bags for my birthday.

Those toys mostly got broken or lost, but I loved them anyway.

When I was in my sleeping bag, I said a prayer full of Gratitude Attitude. While I was at it, I prayed that maybe Simon could disappear.

CHAPTER 25

Powerful Prayer

The next morning, when I got downstairs, Mom was sitting at the table, staring at her coffee cup. Brown, round things were sitting on a plate. Mom used to say, "I'm a great history professor, not a great cook."

"What are those?" I asked.

"Potato pancakes." Mom nodded her coffee cup toward the plate. "You remember potatoes?"

I'd sure seen enough of them come into this house. "I remember potato chips," I said. "I remember baked potatoes with Dad's special sauce." I looked at her face and added quickly, "Now I'll try potato pancakes."

While I nibbled, I told Mom, "I changed my mind—I do not want to go to school in Oakwood."

Her eyebrows stayed calm. "What will you do all day?"

Oh, I had plenty to do. But all I said was "Help with Isabella."

"How do you plan to make friends?"

Mom and Dad didn't believe me no matter how many times I said I didn't really need friends. "I think Isabella misses preschool," I said.

She reached out and combed the ends of my hair with her fingers. "How about you? Do you miss school?"

"Mo-om." Isabella's voice floated down from upstairs.

While Mom squeaked up to get Isabella, I thought about it. I missed the tiger salamander and the caterpillars and my safety poster with the gold ribbon on it. I missed the same-sames the way they were before. But not school in general.

Too bad I couldn't be Morgan in her tree house school.

While Mom showed Isabella yummy ways to eat potato pancakes, I made illustrations for one of my favorite pages in my Safety Notebook: How to defeat Egyptian Chariots:

1. Choose a rocky terrain.

2. Attack the driver.

3. Don't bother to try damaging the wheels because they are too strong.

After a while Isabella came and stood by my chair. "You can use my markers," I said. "As long as you don't massacre any of them. And if you're quiet."

We worked quietly, giving Mom the gift of silence. I liked it that Mom was trying to care about potatoes, but it worried me, too. Dad poked his head in. "Ready to rock and roll?"

I looked up. "Where's Mom?"

"Writing time for Mom."

Good, I thought.

Dad helped us put things away and then swung

Isabella onto his shoulders. "By the way, Simon's grandmother called to apologize for the egg on our door. She's taking him away for the weekend to see if a vacation will help."

Wow. Prayer was powerful. I imagined Simon's bike coming toward me and I was standing there frizzy with light, shouting, "I'm not just a *girl,* you know. The angel Gabriel is basically my *best friend.*"

God was making haste.

CHAPTER 26
୭

Farm Food Forever

All the way to the farm Dad made only one noise—when he rolled down the window and whistled to a hawk sitting on a fence post.

We drove up to the Lavender Fields Forever sign. "Wow," Dad said. "Well, farm lunch will still be the same." He smacked his lips. "*Knepp* and *bohne beroggi* and *mak kuchen*."

"What are you talking about?" I said. I always thought he loved Grandma Campbell's cooking.

The car stopped. "Fun, fun, fun," Dad sang. He

helped Isabella out and put his arms around both of us. "Wow."

"What?" I asked.

He turned us until Isabella and I were face out. "The farm used to be a quarter section. That's one hundred and sixty acres—small even in those days and really too small to farm now. But I thought it was huge."

"I *still* think it's huge," I told him.

"It's twenty acres now." He moved us in a slow circle. "My grandparents planted those trees to keep the north wind from blowing snow into the yard. Look how big they are!"

I couldn't wait to tell him about Morgan's tree house. I couldn't wait to be up in Morgan's tree house.

"Clotheslines in the barnyard?" Dad said. "That's not right."

"Did the barn have horses then?" I asked.

"Yes. And cats who hid their kittens there. Also"— he laughed—"your grandma's favorite. Turkeys."

"The barn is closed up now," I told him.

"Sad." He kept turning us. "Wait. *This* is that house that I tried so hard to throw a ball over? I guess I was skinnier than I thought."

As Isabella and I ran up the ramp to the front door, I discovered that farm lunch smelled like vinegar and yeasty bread. Inside, I discovered that Great-aunt Dorcas had gone off to Mary-Martha Circle at the church. Great-aunt Lydia called, "Is that you? Welcome."

We sat down at the loaded-up table, and Dad said the blessing. My hand felt sweaty in Great-aunt Lydia's hand.

Then Great-aunt Lydia filled our plates with *bohne beroggi* and *knepp* and pickles and green beans grown from seeds that came all the way from Russia. "Every year Mama dried beans in the upstairs room," Great-aunt Lydia said. "One day Katherine decided they were in the way of her paper dolls and she should move them onto the roof to dry." She chuckled. "*Ach*, we had to run after those beans."

"Was it always this hot?" I asked.

"Usually not until summer." She poured iced tea

for everyone. Dad gave me a nod to say I could drink it this time. "My mother sat by our beds with a bowl of cold water and fanned the air to help us sleep."

I wanted to be a good example for Isabella and taste everything, but I whispered to Dad that it wasn't exactly savory to eat sweet mashed-up red beans. "Why not?" he said. *"Das schmecht gut."*

Morgan banged through the screen door with Cousin Caroline right behind her. "Mom wanted to bring you lavender honey," she said. "Did you know one of the Spanish Hapsburgs could touch his nose to his chin?"

"What?" I said.

"I read it this morning," Morgan said. "Also, only two kings of England died in battle. Harold and Richard the Third."

"Welcome to our school day." Cousin Caroline moved a piano bench close to the table and sat on it. "Don't worry about us. We've eaten."

"Too bad for them those kings weren't our ancestors," I said. "Our ancestors would have refused to fight."

"Our ancestors were the total opposite of kings." Morgan leaned over my chair. "They were martyrs who died for their faith."

Isabella tugged my arm. "I want more pickles."

I helped her and myself. Morgan swiped a roll. She said, "Before we lived here—when we visited—my cousins always played a game they called persecution. My dad said it got old hearing that Mom's ancestors suffered and were martyred by sword, rope, fire, and water."

The words *my dad* hung in the stiff air. Where was Morgan's dad?

One of the dogs barked outside, making everyone relax. I looked at Dad and raised my eyebrows. "Why didn't you tell *me* about persecution?" I asked.

Cousin Caroline said, "Our ancestors moved from Switzerland to France to Russia trying to stay ahead of rulers who insisted the young men had to serve as soldiers. Believing in 'Blessed are the peacemakers' and 'Love your enemies' didn't make them very popular."

"Russia is a long way from Kansas," I said.

Dad chuckled. "A new czar decided to force the young men to go to war. So whole villages packed their bean seeds and wheat seeds and blue and golden poppy seeds and got on a ship. They felt God was telling them to go to Kansas."

Cousin Caroline held up the bowl of beans as if to say *ta-da*. "Some women wore all their petticoats to make room for the seeds. Bean seeds. Blue and golden poppy seeds. Also red winter wheat. The wheat was a lucky success here."

"Maybe it wasn't luck," I said. "Maybe God rewarded them."

Great-aunt Lydia didn't look like she agreed. I remembered what Dad said about her and church.

"I need another pickle," Isabella said.

"You really are farming?" Dad asked Cousin Caroline. "Isn't that doomed?"

She gave him a look. "I'm keeping a few steps ahead of failure."

I felt sad that Grandma was the reason not enough acres were left for lucky wheat.

Dad's phone rang. Couldn't the church leave him alone for a *minute*? He went into a bedroom to take the call.

Dad, actions speak louder than words.

"Hey." Morgan poked my shoulder. "Want to see something interesting?"

"Me, too," Isabella said.

"You stay and eat more pickles." I hopped right up and ran out after Morgan.

CHAPTER 27

Maybe I *Will* Miss This Place

<u>Safety Tips for Bees</u>

1. Bees sting when they're frightened, so don't swat them or run around. Be calm.

2. Even a dead bee can sting. Wear gloves, and hold the dead bee by the body.

3. If you get stung, stay calm to keep the venom from zinging through you.

4. Scrape the stinger out with your fingernail so it will stop pumping venom.

5. Remember that a bee doesn't want to sting you because then it will die.

When we got outside, Bob-Silver was in the yard with his nose down, sniffing wildly. "Leave it!" Morgan shouted to him. "Probably a rabbit," she said to me.

"Is that the interesting thing?" I asked. "Because I've seen rabbits."

"Nope. But first we get to feed the chickens."

She grabbed a carton of stale cottage cheese sitting on the steps. We ran through the trees to where the hens were in the fenced yard, popping straight up into the air like Ping-Pong balls and pecking at a tree branch. When they saw us, they rushed toward us as if we were famous and this were their chance for autographs. They gobbled the cottage cheese and wiped their beaks on the grass.

Morgan and I laughed so hard we almost fell over.

"Sasha has the best sense of humor." Morgan pointed to a black-and-white hen. "If she gets to know you, she'll rub against your leg. When they were chicks, Mom and I decided to give them a celebration. You should have seen them! Puff balls with beaks and legs and party hats."

I wanted to hear more, but the wind started up, sending empty egg cartons bouncing around and hurtling toward the trees. As we scrambled after them, I heard the odd faint booming sound. "Is that the interesting thing?" I called.

I predicted I was right, but Morgan hollered, "Next stop, lavender. Soon as I stick these cartons in the chicken house."

We raced back toward the great-aunts' house. Morgan leaped over a ditch, so I followed, almost kicking a rosy flower. "Hollyhock," Morgan called as she started to climb the hill by the barn. "The heat must've fooled it into blooming early."

In the heat and wind, I could feel my face turning radish red.

She didn't pause until we were in the middle of the plants lined on the hill—three thousand of them so far, Morgan said proudly.

Lavender didn't boom, but it definitely did buzz. "Did you plant an air conditioner?" I asked.

"Bees."

Uh-oh. The Safety Club had talked about bees that went wild and started stinging people. But I didn't want Morgan to think I was babyish, and luckily, Cousin Caroline was probably prepared for anything.

"Mom and I weed and mulch and prune and harvest lavender all by hand," Morgan said. "In June we're going to have our first Lavender Festival. Want to help?"

Yes—except I'd be back in Colorado. "Was your mom really a cop before she was a farmer?" I asked.

"Search and rescue cop and trainer of K-nine dogs to help." Morgan picked a bud and held it up to my nose. "The lavender is blooming early, too."

"By the way," I said into her hand, "where is your dad anyway?"

"That's private." She turned and kept climbing.

Divorce? Died? I hiked after her to the top of the lavender hill.

For a minute we let the breeze at the top cool us. Then we plunged down the steep slope of the other side, pushing through woody bushes that grabbed at us. "How do you keep from getting lost?" I was panting.

"You haven't even seen our part of the farm yet. Ow!" Morgan slapped a branch that had smacked her.

What had Cousin Caroline been like as a girl running with Dad chasing her? I almost bumped into Morgan's back. "Sorry," I said. "Didn't realize you stopped."

"This used to be pasture, but it got overgrown." Morgan stood on her tiptoes. "See that fence? It's the end of the Stucky land now."

At the bottom we were suddenly in grass and dandelions, and then I saw the pond! "North Emma Creek wanders through this pasture," Morgan said.

"The same North Emma Creek in Oakwood?" I asked.

"Of course." She twirled around, arms out. "Most of the creek isn't on our land anymore. But one of our ancestors made this pond. A long time ago."

We splashed our hot faces. I turned over a rock, hoping for a salamander.

"Look," Morgan said. A bird was picking its way

gently through the water as if it were trying to show off its *S* of a neck. Its narrow beak was yellow, and it had a splash of feathers like a ponytail.

"Wow," I said. "Is that the interesting—"

The bird leaned forward. Its wings opened, and it lifted into the air and sailed away with its snaky neck out and long, gangly legs dangling behind.

Wait. It was my angel!

"Great blue heron," Morgan said. "It can nab fish in nothing flat."

What I thought was an angel was really a bird that nabbed fish? I started to laugh. Morgan squatted beside me and poked a rope of spotted frogs' eggs. "We haven't even gotten to the interesting thing," she said.

Up on the hill Cousin Caroline shouted our names.

Morgan stood up and yodeled, waving her arms.

When Cousin Caroline made it through the tangle of plants, she was carrying a small goat. "Isn't it cute?" Morgan asked. "It's like a dog only with four stomachs."

Cousin Caroline set the goat down and pulled burrs from her braid. "Your dad's call was from your

mom," she told me. "He went to help."

I felt a thump-thump of nervousness. "Where's Isabella?"

"Taking a nap with Lydia. Morgan, we've got egg customers coming. Will you get things ready? And get this bold baby back in its pen?"

The goat bleated as Morgan thumped off. Cousin Caroline bent to pick a plant. "Watercress. Try it."

I nibbled the stem, feeling like a goat myself.

"We eat those cattails, too." Cousin Caroline pointed to green spikes in the middle of floppy stalks that looked like they'd been trampled by winter. "Wait until you see the summer seeds bursting out and floating down like stars. If I were lost in the wilderness, I could survive better with a cattail pond than with a catfish pond."

I scooped up a tadpole, feeling life wiggling in my palm. "Do blue herons bite?"

"They throw up on invaders that get too close to their babies."

My angel threw up on people? I giggled.

Cousin Caroline wiped sweat from her forehead and helped me up. "Everyone says these acres are too hilly and too rocky to farm. But I'm stubborn."

When we were at the top of the hill and looking down on lavender plants again, my arms were scratched, my knees were still damp from kneeling by the pond, and the wind had picked up my hair and was whipping it into my face. But the air smelled sweet green, and I felt full like I'd swallowed joy—the Christmas-angel-to-all-people kind of joy.

Somebody bellowed. Morgan running uphill toward us with her face red and hot. "Isabella," she panted out. "She's gone." She looked at our faces. "No. Really."

CHAPTER 28

ⓒ

Searching for Isabella

A day could go from good to bad so fast! "Great-aunt Lydia and I searched the house," Morgan said. She grabbed her mom's arm. "I shouted as loud as I could."

Cousin Caroline was instantly on the move. "Don't panic."

"Wait." I rushed after her. *What if . . .*

Back in the house, Great-aunt Lydia was twisting her hands together. "Don't worry," Cousin Caroline said. "We'll find her."

Don't worry? I had no idea how big an acre was,

but it took about five minutes to walk from the chicken house—and I hadn't even seen Morgan's side of the farm yet. What about the brush and weeds? "You checked all the rooms?" I asked Morgan.

"Under all the beds and chairs and everything."

"She went outside then." Cousin Caroline started for the door.

"Could she have been ambushed?" I asked, hurrying after.

"By what?" Morgan knocked my elbow.

"A rattlesnake?" Rattlesnakes don't want to meet you, I reminded myself, any more than you want to meet them.

We searched in the corn rows and poppy plants and behind the azalea bushes. I even looked in a wheelbarrow. What would look interesting to Isabella?

Cousin Caroline whistled. The dogs barked.

"I tied them in the goat pen," Morgan said. "Bob-Silver gets stuck on the hens."

"The egg customers!" Cousin Caroline clicked her

fingers, sounding like Great-aunt Lydia. "Well, they'll have to wait."

When Morgan untied the dogs, they scrambled over a water pan and shook muddy water on us. The goat danced around as if to say, "Take me, too." Cousin Caroline leaned over TJ, rubbing her hands up and down his side. "Time to work, buddy," she told him. She turned to Morgan. "Take Bob-Silver home and shut him in the house, okay? Grab the harness and bring it for TJ. Hurry."

Oh! K-9 dogs could do search and rescue!

I scanned the farm. From here I couldn't even see the chicken house. Too many trees. "What are those tall, round things?" I pointed.

"Silos. From the wheat days."

"Hollyhock," I said suddenly. "All rosy red in a ditch."

Cousin Caroline nodded. Her braid twitched. "There are ditches everywhere on this farm. But let's check that one at least."

Isabella could have fallen anywhere.

By the time we got to the ditch, sweat was running into my collar, and I felt like the wind was going to shove me in.

The flower stood in the ditch all alone with no Isabella. We could hear a dog barking, though. TJ, coming closer. "Why can't Bob-Silver help?" I asked.

"When I was trying to train him, he took me to small, furry animals as often as he took me to evidence. Come on."

Inside the house Cousin Caroline was all business. TJ was so serious he even tried to keep his tongue inside his mouth.

Hurry. Hurry. My throat was dry and choked. Cousin Caroline wiped a gauze pad on the chair where Isabella had sat for lunch. She held it out to TJ. "Take scent." We followed him around the house— "the scent cloud," Caroline said. Then she opened the front door.

On the ramp the wind blew my hair around, and I pushed it impatiently away with sweaty hands. "Don't run," Morgan told me.

"Why not?"

"I mean if you get bit by a rattlesnake. If you panic, it makes the venom go into your blood faster."

Cousin Caroline gave her a look. "No one's getting bit by a rattlesnake. Best way to survive a rattlesnake bite is don't get bit in the first place. People worry about snakes and forget about things like heat index."

Why had I gone off with Morgan instead of watching Isabella? Why?

While TJ zigged and zagged across the old barnyard, Cousin Caroline talked comfortingly about people TJ had found—lost hikers: a guy who had stolen a television and tried to escape through thick woods; a toddler who had wandered away.

Please, God, keep Isabella safe. Big things could get you, like hurricanes. Little things, like heat index, could get you, too.

Never give up hope.

TJ put his nose down. Cousin Caroline nodded. "Now we're off."

Why hadn't I stayed right beside Isabella?

TJ led us straight to the barn and put his paw on Cousin Caroline's knee. "Good, clever dog," she said, bending over to give him praise rubs.

"But it's closed up," I said. "Are you saying Isabella could be in here?"

"Yesterday I was thinking about drying lavender bundles in the attic." Cousin Caroline hurried over to the door and gave it a fierce pull. "Wind must have slammed this door shut, and I guess the latch fell down inside and locked it."

Oh, no, oh, no, oh, no. We had found her, but we couldn't *get* her.

"There's a side window broken out," Morgan said. "I can get in that way."

"Me, too," I said quickly.

Morgan led us to it, and Cousin Caroline checked for any jagged glass. Then Morgan went in, and Cousin Caroline hoisted me up, and for a second I rested my stomach on the old sill. Then over and down.

The barn smelled of straw. I squinted. Thousands of thick spiderwebs. A dangling rope with a knot. Old leather harnesses. Isabella's coughing floated with the dust.

"Mom," Morgan called, "run and get some water."

I stumbled over rough boards and flung my arms around my sister. "Isabella! We found you—TJ did!"

"Go away." Isabella was shaking. "You went *off*!"

I knew she didn't mean it. I knew she was embarrassed and scared, but it hurt my feelings even if maybe I deserved it. "Forgive me." I said it silently but with a pure heart. As pure as I could anyway.

A hen squawked. Morgan knelt in the dust and slid a finger under its beak. "It calms her right down," she said. "Look, Isabella. Did you follow Pinky in?"

Isabella held out her arms to Morgan. Not to me.

I'm sorry I didn't keep you safe, I wanted to say. Maybe a call from God was too much for a nine-year-old. Even if I was almost ten.

CHAPTER 29
❧

The Biggest
Door Slam Ever

Morgan picked Isabella up, and I stood beside them in the shabby old barn, hugging my shoulders. "Great-aunt Lydia used to bring our grandmas here to feed the horses," Morgan said. "She told them horses like hay the way people like *knepp*. We could try to figure out the latch, but it's easier to just go out the window."

As we groped across the barn, I thought about Great-aunt Lydia twisting her hands. "I don't think she believes God watches over people," I said.

"Because she heard so many scary family stories

when she was little," Morgan said. "The church burning. Faith, Hope, and Charity."

"Were they triplets?" I asked.

"Cousins."

"Got the water!" Cousin Caroline called. "Send her out!"

Morgan lifted Isabella through and then laced her fingers so I could step into them and up. When I was out, I blinked in the brightness. Isabella was leaning into Cousin Caroline and slurping from a cup.

"Isabella?" I reached for her.

She burrowed into Cousin Caroline.

Just then I saw our car pull around the curved driveway. I saw Mom and Dad get out and rush uphill toward us. In a couple of minutes Dad was scooping Isabella from Cousin Caroline, saying, "I thought she was fast asleep."

"We found her." The words flapped out. "TJ did it. She was chasing Pinky, I think. Probably she hated the spiderwebs." I tried to rub Isabella's back as we walked.

Mom was talking to Cousin Caroline. I heard

"Colorado." I knew it! Mom was done with this experiment. "My dad is in the hospital," Mom said.

Wait. I turned. Grandpa in the hospital? Was *that* the way the power of prayer was supposed to work?

I ran back and grabbed Mom's arm. "In a minute," she said. "Let's say our good-byes."

Good-byes. Wow. I was leaving Kansas right now.

At the house Dad ran in to get Great-aunt Lydia. I leaned on the car, breathing great lungfuls of dust and heat. "Do you want me to get you a pickle?" I asked Isabella.

Isabella buried her head in Mom. "Give her a minute," Mom whispered to me. "Everything will be okay."

It would be perfect. When we got home to perfect Colorado.

Dad came out the door, pushing Great-aunt Lydia in her wheelchair. My brain wanted everything to slow down. Where was Morgan?

With the egg customers probably.

Would I ever see her again?

"Thank you for rolls and pickles," I said as I kissed Great-aunt Lydia. "Thank you for the rescue," I told Cousin Caroline as I got in my seat. "I don't think your farming is doomed."

She leaned in and kissed me. "You're all welcome here anytime."

"You won't be able to get rid of us," Dad said, climbing in.

What? Something dark and scared swirled around inside me, even though I couldn't give it any kind of name.

Good-bye. Seat belts on? Car rumbling. *What if* . . . I leaned forward. "Are you guys . . . you know. Because if you are, I will never, ever, ever forgive you."

Dad started the car.

Our family was coming apart. What could I do—and quickly?

Dad eased the car past the sign. "Mom and I aren't getting divorced if that's what you mean, Anna. This trip to Colorado will probably be quick."

"Grandma could use some help," Mom said. "That's all."

My brain whooshed with relief.

Isabella wailed out and kicked the seat. Dad called out, "Stop. Isabella! You're going with Mom."

"I am, too," I said.

"I'm sorry, Anna," Dad said. "You're not."

"What?" The air roared, and I could barely hear Dad saying that I needed to calm down and "Isabella, could you please *stop*?"

No! This was bad—really bad. "You need me," I told Mom. "So does Isabella. We should stick together."

"You and I can manage just fine after school," Dad said. "You'll want time with your own friends."

"I don't have friends! I don't need friends!"

"You'll have friends soon," Mom said.

Step one, I thought. Be calm. *Maintain cool*. I took deep, calming breaths until the car pulled into our driveway and we got out. "Help me gather my books I need so I can keep going on my journal article, okay?" Mom hugged me. "I'll try to keep going on it if I can."

I hung on. "I'm good at stapling your papers. I can cook. Anything!"

"Oh, honey." Mom walked me inside the house. "You're very capable, but you're not our indentured servant. We want you to have time to play."

"But I—"

"Anna. Please. Give me a few minutes to get packed up."

"There's no point!" I yelled. "The experiment is *over*!"

Mom combed my hair with her fingers. She claimed she couldn't even remember she'd said "experiment."

"Anna." That was Dad calling. "Can you come upstairs?"

I jerked away from Mom. "No!" I hollered it as loud as I could. No more maintaining cool. "Enough temporary!"

"Oh, Anna." Mom's voice frizzed. "Temporary can be six months or even a year."

A *year*? A year of a pink room? A year of Simon? When Grandpa was sick and Mom and Isabella would stay with him and Jericho would probably be graduated?

Dad came midway down the stairs. "A great thing about being a kid is that you don't have to worry about things adults worry about."

But when I worried, I got prepared. And that was good.

Dad took another step down. "You help me take Mom and Isabella to the airport tomorrow morning. Then have fun in school."

Fun?

I stomped over and pushed past him up the creaky stairs. The air wobbled around me. If God watched sparrows and me and everything else, I would show God the biggest door slam ever.

CHAPTER 30

❧

Gandhi Wouldn't
Make Me Go to School

Early the next morning I woke up to Dad kneeling by my sleeping bag, giving me a big, squishy hug. I made myself unsquishable. "Get your school clothes on," he said. "I'll take you right after we get back from the airport. I have a meeting at the church, but I can get you all set first."

Nonono. We should stay together. What if Grandpa needed more help than anyone thought? What if Mom and Dad decided they deep down belonged in two different states?

In the car heading out of Oakwood toward the

airport, I looked at Isabella. She was in her car seat, sucking her thumb with her eyes closed.

The air was muggy and heavy, and I missed clean, dry Colorado air.

I stared out at the grass. Was it possible to hang on so tight that Mom would have to peel me off one fingernail at a time? "How about a family vote?" I said. "Who's in favor of staying in Kansas and who's not?"

Isabella sniffled and looked away.

"Sorry," Dad said. "Families aren't democracies."

"That's not fair. Martin Luther King and Gandhi wouldn't be forcing me to stay here without Mom."

"Anna . . ." He sighed. "We all have jobs. Mine is at this church right now. Mom's is with Grandpa and Grandma right now. Yours is to go to school right now."

But I could do much more helpful things than go to school.

We pulled up to the terminal. "Families that got separated in covered wagons had to leave messages pinned to sticks or tucked in hollow trees," Mom said.

"Isabella and I will be a phone call away."

I had no more plans or ideas and only enough time to kiss the two luckiest ducks good-bye. When Dad asked if I wanted to move to the front, I said, "No, thank you. The backseat is the best place for someone my age."

"Oh," he said. "Thanks for reminding me."

All the way home I rested my head against the window, trying to cool my brain. "Dad," I said. "When you visited Kansas, did they tell stories of Faith, Hope, and Charity?"

"Uh-huh. Three girls born when no one knew if the community would survive here." He shook his head. "Babies almost always give people new hope."

"Their teacher never should have let them go," I said.

Grassy fields flew by outside.

A farmhouse.

A cow.

"Dad," I said, "how can I help you with the hump?"

"You can maintain cool about school."

Did he think people might judge *him* if he let me stay out of school? How massively unfair was that?

When we got to Oakwood, Dad parked in front of the school. I got out, all draggy shoes. "Hey, look," he said as we went up the steps. "Tornado safety poster." I didn't bother to tell him I was already prepared.

I looked at the gray floor. Down the hall. Into the school office. Dad said, "I'll be here to pick you up right after school, Anna."

The secretary behind her desk shook her head. "You don't have to do that. Except for the rural bus riders, everyone pretty much walks home together. Your home is on Cole, right? Very close."

How did she know who I was and where I lived?

"I'll be here," Dad said.

I watched Dad scribbling on the forms she handed him. I shuffled closer to the office door. Outside the school, I heard two small boys calling to each other. Closer, someone clomped up a staircase. At the desk the secretary tap-tapped on her computer.

I was like a piece of paper waiting to be written on. Completely unprepared.

Dad hugged me good-bye. I followed him out to the hall. I put my hands over my eyes and heard a phone ringing behind me in the office and his footsteps fading, and I smelled dust mops and old bananas. This was *not* my school. *My* home was *not* on Cole. "Be with you in a sec, Anna," the secretary called.

I crossed my arms. God had been no help.

Time for Plan B.

"Forget it," I told God. I'd handle things on my own.

I tiptoed down the hall, out the door, down the steps, and scurried behind a big bush all pink with flowers.

One-one hundred. Two-one hundred. Sweat trickled down my back, making me itch. How could I itch at a time like this?

The door opened. The secretary poked her head out and looked all around.

I stayed folded and silent behind the bush. Something pink was helping me for a change.

"Anna?" she called. "Did her dad take her after all?" she asked herself. The door closed.

I started running toward home.

Actions speak louder than words.

CHAPTER 31

The Running-Away
Plan

<u>Safety Tips about Clouds</u>

1. Gray clouds that look like gravy can bring rain, especially if they look wet.

2. Puffy gray clouds and warm, moist mornings can bring a thunderstorm late in the afternoon.

3. When you see an anvil shape, the storm usually moves in the direction the anvil is pointing.

4. Watch out for flat clouds getting lower or puffy clouds getting higher.

5. Our ancestors said if you see a thunderhead cloud, it's time to pause and consider the majesty of

God. If the cloud has a funnel coming down, it's time for a picnic in the root cellar.

I tore toward my house, wishing that Mae and Slurpee were here with me today. I should have told Slurpee about Isabella. Why hadn't I said, "Come on over to play"? I hadn't tried hard enough to help Isabella adjust.

As I raced over the North Emma Creek bridge, I hoped people weren't looking out their windows. I hoped the secretary would take a few minutes to find Dad's phone number. I hoped the door was unlocked, and it was.

For a moment the silence of the house shocked me. *Mo-om*, I wanted to wail. Like Isabella.

I raced up the squeaky stairs to my bedroom and grabbed my backpack and stuffed things inside. Hat. Sunscreen. Safety Notebook. Midnight H. Cat was purring on the bed. I scooped her up, all warm and floppy, and stood there with my arms full of cat.

She'd hate being in a backpack.

Slowly I let her back down. *Oh, no, Midnight H. Cat.* Time for a plan.

1. Get to Colorado.
2. Somehow.
3. Figure out how to get Midnight H. Cat there, too.

I heard a car sound. Dad? "Good-bye," I whispered. "I will definitely save you." I kissed my cat and grabbed my backpack and rushed downstairs and peeked out the door. Not Dad. Yet. Even though Old Kickapoo cannon was slamming in my chest, I pounded up the sidewalk with my backpack bouncing.

All the way to the sign, I felt like Daniel in the lions' den and Gandhi on his nonviolent salt march all rolled into one brave—or desperate—girl.

Un-welcome to Oakwood.

Then I stopped. What was I doing?

But I knew how to stay safe. I wouldn't let any strangers see me. I walked faster with all my senses on alert.

No sidewalk now. I listened to the crunch-crunch of my shoes on gravel. I caught a faint sound of a car. I hastily shoved through scratchy weeds and crouched.

One, two, three. Just get to ten. Good thing I'd read about rattlesnakes in my booklet. Gray clouds were stacked on the horizon. Good thing I knew about clouds.

Eight, nine, ten. The car zipped by. I stood up. My legs itched and stung. I heard a louder rumble. Quick! Back in the weeds.

This one was slower. A truck. A blue truck. With a dent—I *knew* this truck. I rushed out and waved. The truck rolled to a stop, and a window squeaked down. "Anna?" Great-aunt Ruth's voice called. "Need any help?"

Oh, happy day! Would she lend me money for a plane ticket to Colorado?

"You remember me?" She tried to get her face out of the sun so I could see her. "When Lydia brought you by the chicken house for a look-see? Where are you trying to get to?"

I couldn't say "Colorado." Instead, I blurted out, "Need some eggs."

"Hop in." She pushed the door open. "Did you think you were going to walk the whole way? I told you to give me a jingle. Why aren't you in school?"

"Um . . ." I couldn't think what to say. "Do you buy eggs from Cousin Caroline every day?"

"Almost." She chuckled. "An egg is the perfect food."

She shifted a gear and started the truck rumbling again. As I watched her steer and felt the tape on the seat cover scratch the back of my legs, I got Plan B.

There were plenty of egg customers like Great-aunt Ruth. Cousin Caroline could hire me to help and pick lavender and make pies and feed chickens. It probably wouldn't even take that long to earn money for a ticket.

Great-aunt Ruth dug out her phone. "They know you're on your way?"

"Cousin Caroline said come anytime."

"There you go then."

"Thank you," I breathed, full of Gratitude Attitude.

Great-aunt Ruth and I discussed clouds until we chugged right by the sign, LAVENDER FIELDS FOREVER. Wait! Then I realized Cousin Caroline must have her own driveway. Sure enough, I saw another sign. BUY FRESH EGGS, it said. COMING SOON????? "What's coming soon?" I asked.

Great-aunt Ruth winked. "If you don't know, I won't spoil the mystery."

I wanted to tell her I didn't like mysteries.

By the time she pulled into the parking place by the chicken house, I had my speech planned out. Cousin Caroline opened the truck door. "Everything okay?" Great-aunt Ruth asked. She looked from my face to Cousin Caroline's face and back.

"Thanks," Cousin Caroline said. "I can take it from here."

CHAPTER 32

Anna Versus
the Preacher

Great-aunt Ruth blew me a kiss and walked off with
her egg carton. Cousin Caroline led the way to her
house. It looked like it should be sitting in the middle
of prairie grass with buffalo roaming nearby, not next
to a garden of corn and lettuce and peas.

In third grade I had written a report about the
greater prairie chicken with its gray-brown feathers
and orange head. That's what this house reminded
me of. When the deep snows came, greater prairie
chicken dived into snow to stay warm.

Too bad they were almost extinct.

Cousin Caroline gave me a stern ex-cop look as we headed inside. First, I saw the schoolroom—big paper taped to the walls and an oak table with claw feet that looked like they could kick me.

The kitchen was connected through an inside window. As we walked into it, I saw bunches of herbs dangling from the rafters. It smelled like yeast and cinnamon and sweet grass. A sign on the wall said DON'T KISS THE COOK.

Cousin Caroline pointed me to a chair. She grabbed her phone. Was she calling Dad? School? The police?

My speech drizzled away. "I—" I forced the words out. "I really think I should go with Mom and Isabella to Colorado." It sounded kind of pathetic.

She glanced up. "And you took matters into your own hands maybe? Did something dangerous perhaps?"

Cousin Caroline had definitely interrogated criminals.

I dug my notebook out and held it up so she could read the title. "I'm pretty prepared. But if you have any suggestions, I'd be happy to take them."

She put the phone in her pocket. "Follow me."

I followed her into her basement. Canned goods. An emergency radio. A flashlight that didn't need batteries. While Cousin Caroline took down a box, I studied something called a Screamer that let loose with a 120-decibel signal every five minutes. Cousin Caroline glanced up. "That's in case you're trapped under debris," she said.

"What kind of debris?"

"From an earthquake. Tornado. Flood. Water is full of surprises. Creeks flood, and so do streams. Rivers. Lakes. Thunderstorms fill up underpasses."

"Do you ever think about when the tornado almost hit the farm?"

"My mom said she and Katherine wrapped their arms around each other so they'd go to heaven together." She dug through the box. Outside, car tires crunched on gravel. "Are you expecting a visitor?" Cousin Caroline asked.

Maybe Dad. I should have known Great-aunt Ruth would call him.

"Here we are." She handed me a whistle. "If you're ever tempted to wander off again, at least keep this with you."

I hung it around my neck. It was good to have, even if it was a pity whistle.

We climbed back upstairs and sat at her kitchen table. When the door opened, I saw that my dad, who never got mad, looked mad. My heart thumped like a bad tire.

"Anna!" Was he ready to smite me? "You scared people this morning."

"Who called you?" I whispered.

"Who didn't?" He frowned. "The school secretary and the school principal and Mae, who saw you from her classroom, and two church members, who happened to be watching as you passed by, and Mae's mom—because Mae called her to get my number— and my aunt Ruth! When I get back, I imagine I'll listen to messages from all the people those people told, too."

Wow. Everybody sure knew our business here.

Was *Dad* scared for me? Or was he worried about what the church would think?

Me, I thought. *I want it to be me.* In Colorado it would have been me. "I don't want to go to school," I said. "I want to help Mom."

"Anna, even the Gold Ribbon Safety Citizen doesn't have to take care of everything."

Yes, I do, I thought. Why didn't he listen?

Cousin Caroline pulled out a chair, and Dad sat down with a thump. "Everything is hard already," he said. "Why do you have to be so stubborn?"

Why do you have to be so stubborn? I thought.

Cousin Caroline took a pitcher out of the refrigerator. "Lavender lemonade. It'll cool us down." She poured three glasses. Outside, the dogs started barking. "Morgan runs them everywhere," Cousin Caroline said.

"They're good dogs," Dad said. He was calmer.

"School . . ." My voice cracked. He wouldn't understand. "Anyway, the year is almost over."

Cousin Caroline sipped her lemonade, very calm. "I still have Morgan's fourth-grade books. Anna is welcome to join Morgan and me in school. I could use help with the farm, and I have a cot." Cousin Caroline smiled at Dad. "Remember when you and I had cousin sleepovers with Grandpa and Grandma?"

"Apparently I chased you with frogs." Dad sucked on his straw, and the lemonade rumbled. "What about your cat?" Dad asked me. "She'll miss you."

I crossed my arms. I felt reckless and frightened at the same time. If only I were holding Midnight H. Cat.

"Sometimes," Cousin Caroline said, "people need a little time."

I closed my eyes. I knew what was coming next. A squishing hug and Dad telling me to think it over and make the right decision. I squeezed my eyes fiercely. I felt his arms around me. One. Two.

The arms were gone. The screen door banged. What? I opened my eyes. He was really going? Leaving me?

Morgan burst in with the dogs. "What's going on?"

"Anna is going to stay with us a while." Cousin Caroline poured a glass of lemonade for her. "All set with the eggs?"

I wanted her to say, "Good. Two cousins, two together."

"You're letting your dad go away?" Morgan's expression said that was the most unsavory thing she could imagine. Maybe her dad had driven away with her standing there wanting to shout, "Come back."

The dogs crowded around me, and I patted them, glad for their faces—not mad, not disappointed, not puzzled, with big, warm, all-sympathetic eyes that looked the way Dad's eyes used to look in Colorado.

CHAPTER 33

Hanging On
to the Plan

Cousin Caroline set up a cot for me in the basement, and I made up the thin pad with sheets and blankets. My heart felt wrung out like a washcloth.

When I went back upstairs, Cousin Caroline got me on the phone with Mom. It wasn't a good connection, but I heard, "Oh, honey," and "Thank Caroline for me, okay" and "Grandpa and Grandma miss you."

"How is Grandpa feeling?" I asked. I wanted to say, "And Isabella," but I was nervous to hear if Isabella was still mad at me.

"Itchy to get out of the hospital," Mom said.

"Really? You're not just saying that?"

"Nope." She laughed. "He's studying hiking maps."

How I wanted to be in Colorado listening to that old moose story he always told! My brain made a perfect picture of Jericho with chopsticks in her hair, sitting in a tent with Grandpa and Grandma and Mom and Dad singing "Happy birthday to you."

After we said good-bye, I went to join Morgan, who had a big book open at the oak table. "What subject is your worst?" Cousin Caroline asked.

"Math," I said. "My best is science. Did you know salamanders can regrow limbs?"

Cousin Caroline lifted a math book from the pile. "See if you can figure out where you are."

She went into the kitchen. I started to flip pages.

I had to admit to Jericho in my brain that I didn't even really have a plan. When I tried to come up with one, all I could think of was this.

1. Hang on.

2. Be miserable.

3. See if missing us would bring Dad back to his old self.

I flipped more pages. My brain kept asking, "Where are Mom and Dad and Isabella and Midnight H. Cat?" Like the day the wildfires came into the city. One minute people were getting haircuts and going to the dentist, and the next minute the roads were clogged with cars and exploded schedules.

Morgan took out notecards. "Here's a good idea," she said to her mom. "Maybe *B* should be a king who died *boringly* in his bed, surrounded by his loving wife and children."

"What about *beheaded*?" Cousin Caroline was mixing bread dough at the connecting window.

"*H* is already heads of queens."

"What are you doing?" I tried to see.

"Alphabet book of death for my kings and

queens unit." Morgan bent over her paper, blocking me. "Don't look until I'm done."

"Do you have any other gruesome ancestor stories?" I asked her. Silence. "Is there any way to prepare for feral hog attacks?" I asked Cousin Caroline.

She held her finger to her lips to say shh.

I did one fractions problem. I folded a piece of my notebook paper into a teeny envelope.

Boom-boom. That eerie sound. "Hey." I flipped the envelope at Morgan. "You never showed me the interesting thing."

That did it. The story tumbled out as if I were watching a play.

Morgan: "I told Mom if we were going to move to the farm, I wanted animals."

Cousin Caroline: "I said, 'We need animals we can sell.'"

Morgan: "I said, 'What about cows?'"

Cousin Caroline: "Farm families name their cows. Do you have any idea how cute a calf is? I don't know who cried harder when the cows had to be sold—me or Grandpa."

Morgan: "I wanted a horse."

Cousin Caroline: "Horses get into your heart. Buy a horse, it has a home forever."

Morgan slumped on her elbows. "I *really* wanted a horse."

Cousin Caroline plopped the dough in the bowl. "I said we needed something so ugly only its mother would love it. Want to see what we found?"

She started for the door. Bob-Silver and TJ scrambled up, barking. Morgan and I followed. "I saw an ostrich in a movie at school," Morgan said.

Cousin Caroline herded everyone outside. "I researched ostriches. They're fragile. I refused to use my savings to buy expensive birds that would fall over dead."

We headed in the opposite direction from the barn and over a rise. This was what Morgan meant by "our part of the farm."

"How far—" I said, but Morgan pointed, and

I saw the fenced-in area. Blobs of gray and brown with long necks. "What *is* that?" I asked. As we got closer, the blobs turned into huge birds that ran away on flapping legs. One arched its neck and opened its triangle mouth in astonishment.

So this was the interesting thing!

Morgan tugged my whistle playfully. "Ask us if they spit. That's what people asked at the rest stops when we were driving them here."

"Do they spit!" Cousin Caroline and Morgan started laughing. The birds bobbed back to check us out. Their bodies were round and feathery.

"Um . . ." I grinned. "I don't think they spit."

"Correct." Morgan fisted the air. "An emu is a bird, not a llama."

"Wait." I picked up a feather. "You didn't get ostriches, but you did get emus?"

"Correct," Cousin Caroline said. "Ostriches look for a reason to die. Emus look for a reason to live. This is the big-kid pen."

Who said Cousin Caroline didn't have the sense

God gave geese? "They're perfect," I said.

"I hope you're right." She gave me a thin look. "I'd hate to lose this land."

The land that her bones missed? That would be terrible. "You don't have to pay me for being a hired hand," I said.

She smiled. "Thanks, Anna. I'm hanging on by my fingernails." She sounded all desperate and jolly and determined.

Morgan pulled me through a shed to long, narrow pens with one big emu in each. "The adult females make that booming sound whenever they spot something that makes them uneasy, like a coyote." She glanced at me. "Or I guess like a feral hog."

These emus didn't even need a whistle.

We talked all the way back to the house. Cousin Caroline had used her savings and bought two breeder pairs. "Raising them is easy," she said. "Making money hasn't been. Yet. But everything they produce is healthy, and wait until you see how gorgeous the eggs are."

Morgan grinned. "Wait until you see a big kid emu give a karate kick with both feet."

I was changing my plan.

1. Help Cousin Caroline not lose the farm.

2. See if Dad could grow back his old self—like a salamander limb.

3. Have a great time. It served Dad right.

At least there were three of us now—not counting the great-aunts and emus and chickens and dogs.

CHAPTER 34

୦୨

Saving
the Farm

After supper Dad brought my suitcase to the farm. I hid behind the azalea bushes until he was driving away, and when it was too late, I jumped out and hollered, "Come back!" as loud as I could. I was glad he couldn't hear. My ancestors had faced sword, rope, fire, and water. I could face a few nights without my sleeping bag and cat.

When I was lying on the hard cot listening to the scrabbling of dogs' claws on the boards above me, though, I had to pretend I was in my cozy Colorado tent.

The truth was this basement was a very safe place with its Screamer and all.

The truth was it was way better than a pink bedroom.

The truth was . . . I missed my cat.

When I got to the kitchen the next morning, Morgan and Cousin Caroline were already eating. "Cracked wheat hot cereal," Cousin Caroline said, spooning some into a bowl for me. "You'll need a sweater today. About time we had normal April weather."

I glanced at the calendar on her wall.

April 27.

One month until my birthday.

As I ate, I wondered how fast Grandpa might get well. What was Mom learning in her latest research? Were Grandma hugs making Isabella feel better?

Before school, Cousin Caroline sent us over to the great-aunts' side of the farm to check on the lavender plants. We stood on the hillside with TJ and Bob-Silver crowding around us for ear rubs, and I imagined snow blotting out the sun. "Do you think the teacher of

Hope and Faith and Charity hated that she let them go?" I asked Morgan.

"She thought they'd freeze if they stayed in the school."

"I know." Shiverydee. "Some people have terrible choices."

"Would you rather be boiled in oil or pulled apart by wild animals?" Morgan asked. She picked a bud to take back for Cousin Caroline's inspection.

"What about neither?"

"Our martyr ancestors had to choose," Morgan said. "What if the king said you had to be a martyr or renounce God?"

Pretty unsavory. What happened if you renounced God but had your fingers crossed behind your back?

I dodged away from a bee that floated crazily up. My fingertips were full of lavender oil, and my brain was all curiosity. *When your mom was a girl, did she pretend sticks were guns and did our peacemaker ancestors grab them away? Are your mom and dad divorced?*

I kept the words from flapping out because

sometimes Morgan was like the salamander that hid in leaf litter and preferred a secretive life.

We made our way down the hill and back through the trees. I put my game face on and asked, "Do you think cicadas bite?"

"They don't attack people." Even in this shady, spottled place, I could see Morgan's expression wasn't mocking. "If you held one for a long time and it thought you were a tree branch, it might try to feed, but Mom said that would feel like a pin stuck you."

So. I predicted Morgan had asked Cousin Caroline the same thing. It made me wish I were brave enough to show her the Safety Notebook. "I know what you should do if you're being persecuted for your faith and you got thrown to the lions," I said.

"You do?"

Her voice was sincerely interested, so I told her the plan:

1. Don't quail.
2. Take off any animal skin your captors put on

you because it's supposed to make you look and smell like prey.

3. Grab a whip or shield from the weakest-looking handler.

4. If a lion charges, yell as loud as you can.

"Why?" Morgan asked.

"Lions hate loud noises. But don't try to hide." Jericho had said in Safety Club that people were tempted to dive for the wooden doors around the floor of the arena. Unluckily, those led to more wild animals. And you'd give up your chance to be seen as a hero. "Heroes sometimes won a pardon," I told Morgan.

"Our ancestors didn't want a pardon. They wanted to be martyrs for their faith."

Maybe that was the problem. Dad couldn't be his funny, guitar-playing self here where he could feel his ancestors in his bones.

I kept thinking all the way to the house. "Thanks for taking in this stray," Dad would say at Christmas, flinging his arms around Grandpa and Grandma Campbell. I thought he felt perfectly scooped in to Mom's family. But maybe he always missed his true family.

Maybe he liked a place where everybody knew everything about him.

I didn't.

"I don't actually want to go back to Sunday School," I said. "The boys will be full of comments about how I ran away and got everyone in an uproar."

"I don't blame you," Morgan said. "We'll think of something. It can't be that hard."

Morgan + Anna = team! Score!

CHAPTER 35

॰॰

Mystery and
Frustration

Morgan and I soon had our routine down. Morning chores started in the chicken house. After we found all the isolated eggs, we gently lifted the hens that were roosting, took those eggs, and put the hens carefully back.

I now knew exactly how a smooth brown egg felt in my hand.

Back at the house we made the washing water ten degrees warmer than the eggs to push the dirt away from the pores. When the eggs were clean, they went in cartons.

In the afternoon we did it again. And egg gathering was only one of the chores. Farming was hard work, which luckily didn't leave much time for missing things.

I saved up interesting tidbits to tell Mom on the phone—things like "TJ chose his own name. When Cousin Caroline first took the puppies for food and supplies, he kept insisting on going into TJ Maxx until she gave up and named him TJ" or "Did you know people have made jewelry from emu toenails?"

On Saturday we got to wait until nine in the morning to start chores. TJ looked dignified and disgusted when Bob-Silver ran ahead of us, barking. "If you bug the chickens, it's the goat pen for you," Morgan called.

I was learning the chickens' personalities. Penelope was a graceful jumper. Gwendolyn turned her head and listened to us. Pinky was the escape artist, who might lay her eggs anywhere, and sometimes we stepped on them.

"You know what I wish?" I said as we started our

egg hunt. "I wish nobody but evil and insincere people had to suffer. Like Simon."

"Wow." Morgan looked up. She had straw in her hair. "I didn't expect you to be on the Great-aunt Dorcas team about Simon. And where are all the eggs?"

I flushed. "He *attacked* me."

Morgan stood up. "Gwendolyn is hoarding eggs again. We need some decoy eggs. Go tell Mom."

"What does that even mean?" I asked.

"She likes to sit on eggs that she wants to hatch. Once we found her hiding fifteen! And she'll fight us if we try to take them. But we can fool her with wooden decoy eggs."

I trotted off and was almost to the house when a car drove up to the parking area behind me. I stood on the steps and watched.

The passenger door opened. A leg stuck out. It gave me a bad feeling. Then the boy got out.

Simon!

Morgan must have known he was coming even when I was talking about him.

I watched his grandmother come around from the other side and take his arm as they walked to the chicken house. Why did Simon have to come out to the farm?

It's not like I *owned* Lavender Fields Forever, I reminded myself.

My brain was all suspicion, though. Had Morgan got rid of me on purpose? Did she only want to hang around with Simon and his bullyboy tricks? I watched as Morgan gave a carton of eggs to Simon and his grandma. I watched as Simon's grandma put the carton in her car and started off toward the great-aunts' house.

Go with her, I ordered Simon in my brain. *Get completely away from me.*

Instead, Morgan and Simon walked together toward the trees.

Did Simon know I was here at the farm? Was he storing up more mean ideas? Would Morgan stick up for me or not?

I waited, but all I saw was waving leaves on the trees.

The tree house! Why Simon and not me?

"I saw a bear," I wanted to run and tell Morgan. "I didn't even scream."

Had Simon ever seen a bear?

While I was stomping around and flinging rocks toward the corn plants, Cousin Caroline came out. "How come Simon gets to see Morgan's tree house?" I asked.

Cousin Caroline was all brisk face. "Maybe Simon needs to see it."

That made no sense. Why would anyone *need* to see a tree house?

I pulled out my whistle and blew it as loud as I could.

After a minute Cousin Caroline put her arm around my waist. "Simon's dad was my cousin," she said. "He and your dad and I played together here."

When Dad and I stood by the wooden horse, was Dad thinking about being a kid, running in the fields with Simon's dad?

"When everyone else was saying this farming

idea was impossible," Cousin Caroline said, "he was the one who found me a used tractor. I said, 'I was *born* to drive that tractor.' He said, 'The rest of us had to practice driving a tractor.' He helped with my mistakes."

What was it like to die from lightning? In one second did the universe seem lit up and full of the glory of God? "I'm sorry," I said.

"He and Simon helped build the emu pens, too." Cousin Caroline tugged me. "Let's make lunch."

I wasn't ready to go all soft on Simon, who would only take advantage if I did, but I wished I at least had some allowance to give Cousin Caroline to help pay farm bills. I wished I could promise her she would never be defeated.

Who was I kidding, though? I couldn't even fix my own family.

I was like Hansel and Gretel with all the bread crumbs eaten and no path back.

CHAPTER 36

~

Let My People Go

On Sunday, Morgan kept her word. At the steps to the Sunday School room, she whispered, "Hide! Then run back to your house. Oakwood people either go to church or stay inside, so I don't think anyone will see you. I'll tell Mrs. Miller you feel smallpox coming on."

She grinned to show me she was kidding.

I hid in the sanctuary—no one there except the person up in the front practicing hymns. When everyone was in Sunday School, I dashed outside and down Cole Street.

The field was a mass of bluebells, and luckily, the

house still wasn't locked. I flung myself on the rug by Midnight H. Cat and scooped her up. We rolled around together, all dizzy with love, until it was time for me to go back.

While I listened to the opening music, I watched Dad's foot poking out from behind the pulpit. How long had it been since I waltzed around on that shoe? Slurpee hung backward in her pew, giving me two-finger waves until Dad stood up. I squeaked my shoes on the floor, but Dad was concentrating too hard to notice.

"Sorry the sanctuary is chilly today," he said. "Love your neighbor next to you." That made people chuckle. "Or"—he smiled—"make peace with them fast."

I glanced shyly at Cousin Caroline and Morgan, and they both gave me good-neighbor grins, which gave me a warm spot in my stomach and almost made me forget the missing tooth gaps where Mom and Isabella should be.

Dad said, "We think of our hearts as pure and kind, which they often pretty much are. Until someone wounds us. Or until we remember hard things and pain bubbles up."

I could hear people breathing as if their old wounds were hurting.

"This church's struggles of today go back to its yesterdays," Dad said. "Sometimes we choose anger rather than pain."

He was talking about Simon. Throwing that rock.

"Luckily . . ." Dad paused. "Luckily, there are gifts in suffering."

Some people nodded. Some looked grumpy as grit.

"Wounds can make us softer," Dad said. "After all, chickens eat spiders and other insects and turn them into golden sunrise yolks."

My dad used to preach about Martin Luther King and Gandhi. Now he was preaching about egg yolks?

Dad finished by saying it was hard to be pure of heart if our inner lives were a jumble of grudges. When we stood up, Great-aunt Dorcas was supposed to say, "Peace be with you," but I heard her say that she hoped Dad had the good sense not to do "Blessed are the peacemakers."

At the benediction Dad raised his arms. "Life is

short, and we have never too much time for gladdening the hearts of those who travel with us. Oh, be swift to love, make haste to be kind."

It's terrible when your dad is perfect.

On the way home I reported what Great-aunt Dorcas had said about "Blessed are the peacemakers."

"Those have been fighting words around here—and for centuries, for our ancestors." Cousin Caroline pointed her arm like a sword. "You owe everything to your ruler!"

Morgan shook her fist. "You owe everything to God. The Bible says, 'Love your enemies.'"

I was watching another play.

Cousin Caroline frowned. "How can you refuse to fight your country's enemies? Be a patriot!"

"No," Morgan hollered. "Be a peacemaker!"

"During World War One, the discussion got mean," Cousin Caroline said. "The church burned. People still argue over whether it was a fireworks accident or dynamite."

Poor Dad.

"At least tar and feathers are out of fashion." Cousin Caroline winked at me in the mirror. "Try not to worry about your dad. He's got pretty big shoulders."

That afternoon I explained on the phone to Mom about the church sign. "Are you getting time to write your journal article?" I asked.

"Definitely," she said. "I've been doing more research about Kansas pioneers. People wrote that in those dry years the air seemed thirsty and the wind seemed to shrivel the skin. People needed their relatives to send them supplies by train. Only the most stubborn stuck it out."

So Dad was born to stubborn ancestors. "It's May now," I said.

She laughed and said, "Yes, Anna. Stampeding buffaloes wouldn't make me forget your birthday."

That meant Grandpa was truly getting better and Mom would soon be back. Right then I felt a snap, click, rattle of joy as powerful as the Kansas wind.

CHAPTER 37
ര

Watching

Tips for Rattlesnake Safety

1. Encourage harmless snakes to hang around; they discourage rattlesnakes.

2. Don't hike in snake country wearing sandals or no shoes.

3. Step on logs and rocks and not over them.

4. If you get a rattlesnake bite, squirm until the location of the bite is below your heart.

5. If you try to suck out the venom, you could get poison in a tooth cavity or a gum sore, so don't.

ര ര ര

For the next three weeks I watched Dad for changes. Dad watched the congregation for changes. Great-aunt Dorcas and her friends watched the sign out on the corner beside the church.

First, Dad put up BLESSED ARE THE MEEK.

Meek was basically the opposite of Great-aunt Dorcas, frowning at baby bean plants in the garden Morgan planted by the side of the church lawn. I went over before Sunday School and said, "I don't see what you have against vegetables."

"Beauty of the lilies," Great-aunt Dorcas said.

I listened to her friends complain. They had always planted flowers from pioneer gardens here. Each flower had a hand-lettered sign that educated the younger generation.

They didn't sound meek.

Next came BLESSED ARE THOSE WHO MOURN, which I was pretty sure meant Dad was miserable without us, and then BLESSED ARE THE MERCIFUL, which made me think: Have mercy on my cat!

Every Sunday I stuck to my plan and spent half

an hour with Midnight H. Cat in the empty house on Cole Street. Mom's books stayed in their alphabetical order, and when I touched one, my fingers and thumb left five small holes in the dust. Dad's guitar case was dusty, too. The house was pretty much like the abandoned aquarium before the tiger salamander came to live in it.

I was always careful to be back at church on time. Even so, I waited for Mrs. Miller to tell Dad, but every week, when Dad came out to the farm for supper, he didn't say anything about Sunday School. Maybe Morgan had confessed our plan to Mrs. Miller, and she was having mercy on me.

Dad told me Midnight H. Cat was missing me and that a pot of bean soup lasted *way* too long with one person. It didn't surprise me that he was cooking bean soup even with all those casseroles in the house because he always claimed bean soup was the most comforting taste in the world, even though I disagreed. "You know you miss my bean soup," he said.

"Uh-huh," I said. "Right."

"Want to talk about what I did to upset you so much that day?"

It *wasn't* only one day.

"Change your mind?" he asked every time.

"Change *your* mind?" I asked.

I wasn't about to say, "I'm homesick." Was it homesick for Colorado . . . or for Mom or Isabella or Midnight H. Cat? Was it homesick for Dad's rhinoceros laugh? I got to hear it one time: when he got ready to leave and the goat was standing on top of his car.

Luckily, I had important work to distract me.

As soon as the morning dew dried, Morgan and Cousin Caroline and I used grass shears to trim the young lavender. It was noisy with the bees vibrating their bodies to make pollen fall onto them—so they could carry it back to their hive—and the plants whispering sweet, sweet, sweet. We and the bees tried to stay out of one another's way.

When the day got hot and the oil crawled back to the roots, we did school and emu work. Sometimes, when I watched Cousin Caroline pulling a plow behind the tractor, I felt a wild pain as if something had plowed a big hole through the middle of my heart. But mostly I could only think about eggs and grass shears and shovels and taking one more step with a big bag of emu feed. I even had blisters on my hands and heels.

One afternoon Cousin Caroline put my hand on the bump of fat behind an emu's hips. "You're feeling Omega three, six, and nine," she said. "Emu oil."

"What good is emu oil?"

"It's healthy to eat. Healthy for pets. Healthy for your skin." She sounded worried, though.

"Is something wrong?" I asked.

"Just thinking about fireworks. Last Fourth of July the emus ran for hours. I don't want good, healthy birds running off all their fat."

"Could we get them headphones?" I looked into the emu's oval yellow eye. "A soundproof shed?"

She laughed. "Keep thinking."

When we had time off, Morgan and I caught crawdads and frogs. The same-sames in Colorado only had a park where we collected material for the tiger salamander habitat. *Ha-ha,* I thought. *I have an amazing pond.*

I was unsame as could be.

In my brain, Jericho sat pretzel legged, beaming. "I'm helping save a farm," I told her.

She was proud of me.

Now I knew how to listen for a rattlesnake warning: tick-tick-tick, whirr. I also knew snakes couldn't help it that people walked around in their habitat.

The only thing I didn't like was the Saturday when Simon came out to the farm again while his grandma got eggs. While he and Morgan went off to the tree house, I sat on the porch and called Mom.

"Any big wishes for your birthday?" Mom asked me.

"Colorado."

She laughed. "Anything else?"

"You," I said. "And Isabella."

"We wouldn't miss it."

All I needed was *in Colorado.* I crossed my fingers and wished on stars and an abandoned horseshoe. No praying, though. I'd told God, "Forget it." I'd handle things on my own. And I was never going to give up hope.

CHAPTER 38

ᥐ

S Is for Scurvy

When my birthday week finally came, every time the phone rang, I knew it was Dad or Mom saying I should pack my bag for a plane ride. Instead, it was mostly people wanting eggs to make cakes for graduation parties.

"We should have a graduation party," Morgan said to her mom. "I'll do a big presentation of my book." She waved a page back and forth. "We could invite Simon."

"Simon?" I said. "No way."

"I feel sorry for him. Don't you?"

How could I feel sorry for someone who had treated me like lettuce slime?

Morgan got out her markers. "S is for *scurvy*," she told her mom. "But I'm stuck on X. All I can think of is *smallpox*, and that's cheating." She blocked my view with a book.

"Can I borrow your markers?" I asked.

"You're doing math," she pointed out. "Math doesn't have to be colorful."

"When someone's birthday is in two days, everything should be colorful." I looked at Cousin Caroline. "Did you know Gwendolyn collected all the wooden eggs into her nest?"

Cousin Caroline opened a pea pod, tossed up a pea, and caught it in her mouth.

"How did she do it?" I asked. "With her beak?"

She chewed. "Or her feet? I wish I knew."

Morgan frowned. "It's hard to concentrate when people are discussing chickens."

Some people shut up. Others are stubborn. "Why would emus be scared of fireworks?" I asked.

"Fireworks aren't a natural predator of emus."

Cousin Caroline loved talking about the emus. "They hiss as a danger signal. Maybe they think the hissing of firecrackers is some big emu in the sky warning them of danger." She ran her thumb down the middle of a pod, making the peas pop into a bowl. "I don't think they mind the bangs. They never mind my tractor."

I thought of the emus running with their hearts pounding.

"Silly birds," Cousin Caroline said affectionately. "The only danger for them around here is brain worm."

I was about to ask about brain worm, but Morgan interrupted with a pencil chomp. "Do *you* have any good ideas for *X*?" she asked her mom.

"Wax," I said. "King and queen statues in the wax museum."

Morgan gathered her things and banged out the door. I went to the window and rubbed a blister on my palm as she ran across the yard and into the trees.

It was time for me to give up hope about ever being invited to her tree house. Time to give up hope about being in Colorado for my birthday, too. If I were there, Jericho and I would be trying on birthday hats. The only party hats around here were for chicks.

By the time I got up the next day, Morgan was nowhere to be seen, and I gathered eggs by myself.

Who cared? Tomorrow I would have Mom and Isabella. Morgan could spend Saturdays with anyone. It didn't matter to me.

All day I tried not to be sad.

That night Cousin Caroline served a special last-day-of-school supper: emu egg omelets with peas and cucumbers in sour cream and homemade bread and cattail shoots and fried squash blossoms that were thin and slippery and tasted like squash perfume. "Where's Morgan?" I asked.

"She has a commitment," Cousin Caroline said.

My stomach had a terrible ache for three reasons I could think of.

1. Of all my stubborn ancestors, Dad had to be the most stubborn.

2. I was starting to forget the details of my perfect Colorado room.

3. No one here cared about my birthday. Especially not Morgan.

Four if you counted Midnight H. Cat.

After supper, we sat in the living room labeling emu eggs. Last fall Cousin Caroline had let one of the male emu sit on some eggs and hatch them out, but he'd almost murdered one of the females to protect the babies. "Next time," she said, "I'll try an incubator. I'm gathering all the eggs to decide which ones to incubate and which ones to sell. Farmers' market, here we come!"

Holding that football of an emu egg in my hands was like holding the dark green ocean. I was wondering what Oakwood would be like if Grandma had been born in California beside the ocean when a car pulled up. I looked out the window.

Dad! Why?

Cousin Caroline went out to greet him, and I plastered my quivering ear to a crack in the door. "Rain will perk everything up," Dad said.

In the yard Bob-Silver started barking. "Yes," Caroline said, amused. "That's a squirrel. You like squirrels, don't you?"

I imagined myself accidentally sealed up and feeling my way through a pyramid . . . warmer . . . warmer . . . and then I heard my name. "I need to tell her how sorry I am," Dad said.

I flung the door open. "Sorry about what?"

"Hello, Anna." Dad held out his arms. "Lightning damaged airport equipment in Colorado—and about a hundred airplanes. Mom considered renting a car, but the storm front is on the move."

Lightning? Mom and Isabella wouldn't even be here for my birthday?

Outrageous!

How was so much bad luck even possible?

Was God punishing me?

Why? Because of the call? Because I didn't try hard enough?

Dad took a step. His face was in shadow.

Nothing he said could possibly make this any better. I only had one tenth birthday, and it was ruined forever.

Squish squash smoosh splat.

CHAPTER 33
~

Tree House
Disaster

<u>Safety Notebook Questions that Have No Answers</u>

1. Why did the Great Dane get my favorite doll, Miranda, when a doll I didn't care about was right there?

2. Why do chicks have to die before they grow up to be chickens?

3. Why would a tornado hit one farm and skip over another?

4. Why does lightning even exist?

5. Where did all the angels go?

~ ~ ~

For one long minute, I wanted to run to Dad and ask him everything. But how could I? He only cared about one thing now—the Oakwood church. I shoved back into the house and down the basement stairs, wishing I were a species that could give a karate kick with both feet.

Downstairs I paced, with my hands in strangling fists. Cousin Caroline's voice called, "Anna?" Footsteps. "Want to come upstairs? Want to have a Saturday evening soak in the bathtub?"

"I . . ." My fireworks heart was banging. "I'm not even going to church tomorrow." I bumped against a pile of cans that clanked on the concrete floor. "God can be so mean."

Footsteps all the way to the bottom. "Is God in charge of specific weather, do you think?" Cousin Caroline asked.

Who else? Why else did we say, "Holy, holy, holy God of power and might?" Had Dad prayed for Mom and Isabella and my birthday? How did God keep score?

"You might feel better in the morning," Cousin Caroline said.

Her footsteps went back up, and I flopped flat on the bed, thinking about all the questions that had no answers at all.

Birthday morning I went upstairs all draggy shoes. If Mom were here, she'd be making me heart-shaped whole wheat pancakes. Cousin Caroline handed me an egg sandwich. "I've got to dash. Why don't you come, too?"

"Great-aunt Lydia doesn't go to church," I said. "So I don't have to."

"Hurry then," Cousin Caroline said. "I'll walk you over. She's expecting you."

When we got to the azalea bush, I climbed the ramp, and Cousin Caroline headed back. The sky was a gray sheet, and the wind was starting up. What would Dad think when he looked down and saw an empty space where I was supposed to be? What would God think?

"Serves you right!" I said out loud. I marched down the ramp and right to the tree house tree.

For a few seconds I stood there listening. The leaves made a shh noise.

Samson probably felt this way as he wrapped his big muscle arms around a pillar and got ready to pull the building down around him and all his enemies.

I started climbing.

When I got to the top, I wobbled, but I managed to open the door. I stepped inside. A gust of wind puffed the door wide open. I jerked it closed.

Projects were everywhere: crocheted rugs and painted eggs. Angles had been drawn on the walls with pluses and equal signs. A queen with a ruffled collar stared all haughty from the wall as if to say, "What are you doing here?" Beside her, I saw a photo. Two girls with their arms around each other. Morgan had written "My grandma and Anna's grandma" on it.

On the floor were bookmaking supplies. I picked up a page: "*S* is for *scurvy*, which plagued Henry the Eighth, causing great boils to erupt on his legs."

And another.

Q is for the *queens of Henry the Eighth*, whose heads went a rolling across the wood stage.

In a corner, I spotted an album open to a photo of young Morgan grinning with missing teeth, stretching out her arms to catch a kid on the rope swing. The writing said "Simon at the sleepover."

Beside that one was a guy with a pole over his shoulder. "Dad and I went fishing every day." Morgan had drawn hearts around the edges.

I turned the page. Morgan's mom and dad in cop uniforms and TJ in his harness. So her dad was a cop, too. What had he thought when Cousin Caroline decided to be a farmer?

I flipped to the end. I picked up the album to look closer. Morgan's dad. In a different uniform.

A prison uniform?

Outside the house the leaves started fluttering wildly. I crawled over and eased the door open and poked my head and shoulders out.

Rain clicked like dog toenails on the roof. The tree house quivered.

I pulled my head in too fast and whomped the top of it. "Ouch!" I shouted, and let go. The door sprang back open. Thunder crashed, way too close, and wind and rain whooshed inside. I scuttled backward into the corner. *Duck and cover!*

After a minute or so I forced my eyes open. What I saw was awful. A flapping door. Wet pages blowing against the walls and probably outside.

Thunder cracked like God's loud voice saying, "What *are* you doing?"

I scrambled out onto the ladder, slipped down through the wet branches, and raced for the old farmhouse through buckets of rain and smells of wet earth. I burst into the kitchen and practically dived for Great-aunt Lydia and buried my head in her lap. "Why does Kansas have such loud thunder?"

"Thunder." Great-aunt Lydia rubbed my wet head. "That needn't bother a big girl like you. Where have you been?"

I moaned. What was I going to tell Morgan? "I'm mad at God now," I said. "Like you . . ."

A car horn honked, making us both jump. Cousin Caroline shouted, "Anna?" We heard her footsteps pounding up the ramp. The door opened. "I was sent to get you—right now."

"*Ach, jammer.*" Great-aunt Lydia clicked her tongue. "The poor child needs dry clothes."

CHAPTER 40

∾

Surprise

Cousin Caroline hustled me out—where the rainburst had turned to drizzles—and back to her house. "What on earth?" she said, but she didn't wait for an answer. "Run. Get changed. I'll grab a towel and wait in the car."

I clattered downstairs. Was Dad waiting on the steps of the church like Samson with his arms around the pillars, hair bristling everywhere, eyes blazing?

Nah. Dad didn't have hair—or muscles—like that.

Had everyone who came into the sanctuary stared at my empty spot? Had Dad talked about me in his sermon? I made sure my whistle was around my neck and ran upstairs and out to the car. I was in deep, deep trouble.

Cousin Caroline drove fast as I worked to towel-dry my hair. "Is . . . um." I couldn't think what to ask.

"You'll see." She was an ex-cop after all.

"Did you hear anything about Mom?"

She nodded. "They'll be on a flight tomorrow morning."

I crossed my arms. "There sure are a lot of disasters in the world."

She nodded. "Search-and-rescue people say you never know what it'll be. Soon as you prepare for one thing, something else comes along."

That was massively unfair. It was.

What about people who thought nothing at all was coming and didn't get prepared? What about all the people of Pompeii baking bread until *fwoomp*? Volcano ash covered them.

Turkeys thought life was all crunchy grain and sweet water and then *wham*. Thanksgiving.

"There's a comb in the glove compartment," Cousin Caroline said.

I jerked at the tangles in my hair. My brain felt tangled, too.

The church lot was still full of cars. Everyone was waiting to frown at me in unison? Cousin Caroline parked, and I opened the car door.

Suddenly Dad was right there, and I said, "I—" but he turned me around and put his hand over my eyes and walked me along. Scuff. Scuff. Was Dad going to *execute* me?

"Whoa," I told myself. "Maintain cool." He zipped his hand away.

Great-aunt Dorcas was standing by long tables in the middle of the churchyard, tying a plastic hat on. Chairs had balloons floating from them. Someone I didn't know was trotting up the basement steps with a trayful of watermelon.

The next moment people popped from behind trees. "Surprise!" they shouted. "Happy birthday!"

Dad squished me in a hug. "Late to your own party?"

Morgan ran up. "I decorated all evening and before Sunday School." She panted. "You didn't even come to church. Eat quick so it doesn't rain on the balloons."

While she decorated, I was ruining her things.

Good thing the angel with the stick to whack evildoers with was on the other side of the church. I was anything but pure of heart.

"Start the potluck off, young lady," Mae's mom said, handing me a plate.

The fourth-grade Sunday School boys crowded around. "You have a whistle," said Chad.

Another boy shoved him. "I think she might know that."

I actually laughed.

He did, too. "I'm Noah," he said. "In case you forgot."

Great-aunt Ruth came, pushing Great-aunt Lydia in her wheelchair. "Should you be out in this weather?" Dad asked.

"I guess eighty-one means I think for myself." Great-aunt Lydia winked at me.

Everyone ate fast. Slurpee ran up to show off her new screaming monkey. Kylee and Mae plopped down. Mae said, "You're going to have a Lavender Festival in June? Can we help?"

Morgan looked at me. "What do you think?"

I could almost forget what Morgan would say once she saw the tree house.

Almost.

A church door opened, and Dad carried out a cake with fat chocolate frosting like a lawn of sugar. "Want a piece?" Morgan called.

I turned. Who was she talking to? Simon! Lurking around the hedge. Luckily, when he saw me looking, he ran off.

"Let's sing," Dad called.

"Hang on," I said. Simon was at my party and Midnight H. Cat wasn't? I grabbed Morgan's arm. "Will you help me?"

We got to the house in about nothing flat. The cat carrier was right where I'd last seen it, and my cat was purring on the bed. "She used to follow Jericho and me around the block all the time," I told Morgan. "It's just for a few minutes anyway."

We hustled back holding the cat carrier between us. "Put her right by my chair," I said. "It's her first birthday party experience."

"*Now*, let's sing," Dad said.

The last notes were barely out before Great-aunt Ruth called, "You kids eat your cake fast and help us clean up—before this sky lets loose."

I took a nibble and made um-um noises to Midnight H. Cat. Yummy! Mom would have used carrots and sunflower seeds as main ingredients.

By the time I was scraping the crumbs off the plate, the wind was rattling the branches of the hedge. Noah and Chad started lugging a garbage barrel over to a table. A gust swirled paper plates and napkins across the yard.

People grabbed big dishes and leftover food and began to filter away, calling, "Happy birthday," and, "See you!"

I knelt on a chair and stared into Midnight H. Cat's

eyes. She didn't have a real birthday—not one I knew anyway. "You can share mine, though," I whispered.

"Let's get you home," Cousin Caroline called to Great-aunt Lydia over the rising wind.

I looked around. Dad was at the corner changing the letters on the sign. Great-aunt Dorcas started toward him. I scooped up a plate the wind had dumped over. I stepped toward the garbage barrel with a gnawed chicken bone in my hand and an awful thumping in my heart.

CHAPTER 41

୬

Tornado!

Dad sure liked Sunday afternoon routines. He bent and picked out a letter. Put it into its slot on the sign. I stepped a step closer. BLESSED. ARE. THE. P-E-A-

"No call to stir things up even more," Great-aunt Dorcas said.

Shiverydee.

Cousin Caroline, pushing Great-aunt Lydia's wheelchair, stopped.

"Hold on," Dad said. "People like Gandhi and Martin Luther King and Moses . . ." Dad paused. "Hard history doesn't go away simply because you don't talk about it."

But Great-aunt Dorcas didn't want to hold on. "We asked you to help heal problems, not open up old wounds."

"A time for every purpose under heaven," Great-aunt Lydia said. "A time to bind up and a time to tear down. Like Katherine said."

"Katherine!" Great-aunt Dorcas looked like she would shake her fist at the dark sky. "Sneaking off to meet that Nickel boy in the city. Then they were gone—just like that. Broke our mother's heart entirely."

"Oakwood isn't right for everyone," Cousin Caroline said.

Great-aunt Dorcas wagged her finger. "Katherine broke *your* mother's heart, too. No wonder she died young. No wonder you had to go off to be a cop and marry a no-good man whose crimes ended him in prison."

Everyone was talking at once. Cousin Caroline was saying the word *judgmental* and Great-aunt Lydia was saying *ach, jammer* and Morgan's voice was loudest, saying, "He is *not no good*." Angry words rolling, gathering up dirt and flinging it everywhere.

Why did the Christmas angels even sing tidings of great joy, which shall be to all people? The world was still a mess!

"Stop!" Dad shouted. Everyone got instantly quiet. "I wanted to help." I'd never heard him mad like this before. "But everyone would rather hang on to hard feelings." He popped his fist into his palm. "Fine. I leave you to them!"

Whoa. What about the call? I fingered my whistle nervously. It's terrible when your dad isn't perfect.

Great-aunt Lydia rocked back and forth.

I had what I wanted. Didn't I? "Do you mean—"

"Yes." Dad picked up the box. "Let's get out of here."

Cousin Caroline's hand flew up. "No," she yelled. "Simon, stop."

I whirled around. I saw Simon with his hand on the cat carrier.

A fork of lightning stabbed the sky.

The world went wild. Midnight hissing. Rain starting down. My cat leaped from the table and streaked away.

CHAPTER 42

Midnight H. Cat, Where Are You?

I tore after my cat—through the parking lot, toward the houses of Oakwood. Midnight H. Cat zigged and zagged. She paused. Crouched. Footsteps pounded, and from the corner of my eye I was pretty sure I saw Simon. My cat bounded forward and ran.

"Midnight!" My feet slapped against the sidewalk. The edges of my mind realized how creepy green the sky had gotten. A thin, faint siren started wailing.

That stopped me flatter than flat.

The air was thick, and the siren held its breath.

I looked up. Eerie and dark. The wailing that had sighed down to nothing started again.

"Anna." Dad's voice, shouting.

No. I had to get Midnight H. Cat.

"Anna!"

"No!" I hollered over the wind.

"Anna!"

The world went all whirly-swirly.

Hail was pinging and stinging and cracking off cars. The siren wailed. I felt Dad's arm go around my waist, joggle me off my feet. "Dad, wait!" I screamed.

Dad hoisted me up. The downpour crashed onto us. Now my stomach was smooshed against Dad's shoulder, and I felt the ground rumbling and Dad's feet pounding. Door. Dad swung me down and shouted, "Go!"

I was stumbling. Stairs. *Run. Duck.* I was a gladiator, and the beasts howled.

I was almost at the bottom. Bricks—heaving. Table. I scrambled and clawed along the floor. *Run, duck, and cover.*

The lions let out one tremendous roar. My ears popped.

Crash!

The taste of dust choked me. I was coughing and gasping. I groped for my whistle and blew as long and loud as I could.

CHAPTER 43

Luckily, Unluckily

It was dark, and my ears rang.

I coughed and shivered. Where was I? Where was Dad? Had we been blown to bits?

Silence. I could hear breathing. Mine. I reached out and touched a wall.

I was sealed in pyramid darkness.

I was with Hope, Faith, and Charity under a bank of snow.

Silence. Then I heard a faint scrabble. I scratched at whatever was blocking me in.

In a minute someone else's fingers touched mine.

Slice of light. Someone was pulling the wall away. Fingers closed around mine. More scraping sounds. Finally I could squeeze out.

I was lugged up the stairs I'd rush-tumbled down. Out into the air. Set down. Dad was there, kneeling, facing me. I leaned into him.

The next minute people were all around us, talking in blur words. Unluckily, the tornado didn't skip over Oakwood. Luckily, it wasn't a monster tornado. Unluckily, Dad and I were in the wrong place. Luckily, a house was unlocked. Unluckily, Dad didn't have time to get into the basement. Luckily, a fireman lived right next door. Luckily, I had my whistle.

Did it all come down to luck after all? Or was God's eye on the sparrow and me?

Dad had one arm dangling in a weird way. I slumped against him and heard him asking, "Anybody badly hurt? Do we know? How'd the church do? How many houses hit? Anyone know?"

The air still felt thick, and my brain was a fuzzy blanket. My hair was wet. I stumbled a few steps away through floating insulation ripped out of someone's house.

I'd been doing something important.

Midnight H. Cat.

A guy was standing by a car that was upside down with its wheels in the air. A woman walked up to stand by him. "That's a misery," she said.

"Have you seen a black cat?" I asked them.

Mae appeared out of nowhere. "Can I help?" she asked me. She turned to the woman. "Mrs. Yoder, do you have a flashlight?"

Mrs. Yoder patted my shoulder. "Have you checked your own house, hon? Cats have amazing instincts for getting home." She pointed at Dad. "And I'm driving *you* to the clinic right now."

Dad and Mae and I got into her car and rumbled the few blocks to our house, but I couldn't get my brain working. "Look. Your tree isn't uprooted," Mae said. "I'll help you while your Dad goes to the clinic."

The minute I was out of the car, I started calling. *"Kitty, kitty?"*

"Back in a jiffy," Mrs. Yoder called as they drove away.

Mae and I poked and called everywhere. We were calling by where the wind had knocked the shed in the backyard into a jumble of boards when we heard the car come back. Dad's voice was shouting, "Find anything?"

When I got to him, I held up the green jingling mouse. "Just this." All that was left of Midnight H. Cat. My legs were shaking like painful stumps. "Are you okay?"

"A sprain." He held up his sling.

I sat on the porch while Mae helped Dad put Band-Aids on my scratches. The air had a sick-sweet gas smell to it. No wonder my head was fuzzy.

Two Oakwood houses were destroyed, Dad said— the ones that were hit by the vortex. Luckily, they were empty. Other damage was from wind and flying debris.

"Our family?" I held my breath. "The farm?"

The great-aunts and Cousin Caroline and Morgan

were okay, but they were still in Oakwood. "There's a tree across the road," Dad said. "So they haven't been able to drive out to the farm yet."

Pretty amazing everyone was fine, considering that my family had been standing in the churchyard shaking their fists at God and yelling at one another.

Had Dad really said we were leaving Kansas? I turned Midnight H. Cat's favorite cat toy in my hand and tried to remember my terrible tenth birthday from start to finish.

All I wanted to do was climb into my sleeping bag.

Hope was soaking out of me faster than I could stuff it back in.

CHAPTER 44

೧೦

My Guardian Angel, Where Are You?

Early the next morning Mae rang the bell, and Dad gave me a one-armed hug and said she and I could keep looking for my cat while he went to the airport. "Can you drive?" I asked.

"Yep. I'll steer with my right arm and hold the other one still." He climbed in the car, and I stood waving until the car was gone.

I still couldn't believe the only thing left of my cat was a toy in my pocket. And I really wished my angel hadn't turned out to be something that nabbed fish.

Mae and I headed over the bridge. A block away

Great-aunt Ruth was talking to a man. "Funnel pulled back up in the cloud," she was saying. "Touched down a mile away. Picked the roof clean off a barn and didn't touch the chicken shed. Not a feather out of place."

I ran up to her all heart-thumpy. "Has anyone been able to get to *our* farm?" Sasha and Gwendolyn and Penelope and Pinky and the emus? The lavender? All Cousin Caroline and Morgan had worked for?

"Early this morning." She tapped my shoulder comfortingly. "Hardly any damage I hear. I'm heading out there now to have a look-see."

A little damage? Maybe my tree house crime scene might be covered up.

"Let's start where you last saw your cat," Mae said. As we walked, we saw a basketball stand hanging from a tree and an air conditioner sitting in the middle of the sidewalk. We went from yard to yard calling kitty-kitty. People whose names I didn't know said, "Don't give up," and, "Good luck to you, dears."

After a while I told Mae she could be huddled in someone's basement and I should go home to make

signs. While I was getting markers out, I heard the car pull up.

I flew outside and into a four-person hug. Mom kissed me twice. "That's from Grandpa and Grandma," she said. "Let me put on my boots, and I'll help you."

Isabella took my hand. "Daddy told Mommy we're going back to Colorado," she whispered.

"I know," I whispered back. But I couldn't feel anything.

"Anna?" Isabella said.

"What?"

"I wish that cat knew how to run, duck, and find cover. Or I wish that cat had wings and could fly away from the tornado."

"I know."

After they got ready, we headed over the bridge and into town, taping signs on light poles and fences. A man was driving slowly around with cookies and big pots of coffee in the back of his pickup truck, calling, "Anyone need something hot to drink?" At the school Cousin Caroline, smudged and muddy, was helping Noah and Chad and Kylee carry ruined books to a Dumpster.

"The farm's really okay?" I shouted.

"A bit of rain damage," she called back. "No biggie."

Except for the tree house. *No biggie except for Anna damage.*

When we got to the church, I slumped on the front steps by Great-aunt Lydia in her wheelchair. Mrs. Miller and Mrs. Yoder were studying a dented garbage can. Words floated over to us. *How lucky.* Oakwood came *this close* to being flattened. Could have been much worse.

Great-aunt Lydia told me our family's lucky story, too. Morgan and Cousin Caroline carried her up the steps—because garbage cans were blocking the basement steps—and huddled behind a pew. "It sounded like a freight train. Exactly like everyone says," Great-aunt Lydia said. She'd looked up through a window and seen dirt cascading down . . . and then the tornado pulled up, in that weird way tornadoes do, and didn't blow them all to hallelujah.

"What do you think about being saved by a church?" I asked.

"*Ach.*" She winked at me. "Maybe God and I are even now."

Was it luck? Was it God? How did people figure these things out?

I looked around. This church felt familiar now—now that we were *leaving*. Mom was picking branches out of the bean plants. At the edge of the parking lot, Great-aunt Dorcas was frying hamburgers on a camping stove on a long table. Dad was arranging buns with his good hand. "I'm terribly good with onions," Great-aunt Lydia called.

Mrs. Miller came to where we were sitting and pushed Great-aunt Lydia's wheelchair over beside Dad. I didn't have the energy to move or say a word.

A few minutes later hamburger and onion smell was everywhere. Grubby people walked through the parking lot in twos and threes and ate quickly. I could hear bits of conversation about picking neighbors' belongings off bushes and sorting through wet photo albums in living rooms while water still dripped through holes in roofs. "Got a mess back here in the graves," a man called. "Anyone have a free hand?"

Isabella wandered over and settled beside me. "I saved this for you." She opened her hand. "For your birthday." A piece of Kleenex was crumpled on her palm. I took it. Inside was a black jelly bean.

I rubbed her head. "Did you lick it?"

"No. I just kind of slid my cheek on it. You can have my hamburger, too. I didn't put my lips on it." She put her head on my arm. "If I was out there playing with a stop sign, I could have run to the tornado and said, 'STOP.'"

"It's not your fault," I said. "It's mine."

What I wanted was a do-over. I'd never bring Midnight H. Cat to the party.

Or I'd be looking when Simon sneaked up.

Or I'd run faster. Over and over I saw myself catching Midnight H. Cat this time.

What did she think when her world went whirling and twirling—blam?

Isabella's head felt warm on me. "When we cry," she said, "God in our stomach cries."

Would Jericho say even in spite of everything, I should feel Gratitude Attitude? After all, no one was yelling about peacemaking or the sign at the corner. In fact Great-aunt Dorcas was boasting about the emus and saying Morgan had promised not to talk about smallpox and scurvy with customers at the farmers' market.

But why did Simon even come by the church yesterday?

If God was on the side of justice, why did some things end up so lucky and some things so, so massively unlucky?

CHAPTER 45

ꙮ

Smallpox, Tarantulas, and Quicksand, Oh, My

The longer I sat, the worse it was to imagine Midnight whirling through the air. I took Isabella over to Dad and then wandered down the sidewalk, hearing the mocking jingle of the cat toy in my pocket.

We were leaving. Would anyone remember that Anna had been here?

Behind me, a bike squeaked. Who cared? Simon couldn't do anything worse than what he'd already done.

Oh.

I saw it wasn't Simon at all. It was Morgan, with Bob-Silver trotting beside her with his leash hooked to the handlebars. I felt a guilty ache. Morgan climbed off and leaned the bike against a tree. "I waited until Mom left. Because I wanted to bring Bob-Silver along."

"Did you ride the bicycle the whole way?" I asked.

"Got a ride with Great-aunt Ruth to the edge of town." She and Bob-Silver fell in step.

I didn't want to look at her. "It's so great the farm's okay."

"Uh-huh."

It was weird the way tornadoes could hit one block and not touch the next one. I took a breath. "So . . . the wind didn't get your tree house?"

"Something did." Her face made me predict she knew. I wanted so much to say sorry, but I didn't want my apology to be stupid and meaningless. "Do you think tornadoes are the scariest thing in the whole world?" I asked.

"Smallpox is pretty scary," she said. "And scurvy."

"Tarantulas," I said. "For Isabella especially."

"Quicksand. When my mom said we were going to move back to the farm and my dad wasn't coming

along, I thought quicksand might be anywhere."
She twisted Bob-Silver's leash. "I pictured walking
around the farm one day and getting sucked under
the dreadful sand."

I looked at my toes walking. Quicksand. What
good could it possibly do in the world?

We were coming up to Simon's house. I tried to
think how to ask forgiveness from Morgan. How were
people supposed to do it seventy times seven times
when I couldn't do it even once?

"This part of Oakwood didn't get touched,"
Morgan said.

I leaned against the fence around Simon's yard.
The stone animals stuck out their tongues.

Suddenly the fuzz flew out of my brain. I shoved
the gate open. *Simon.* What if he had Midnight?
"Morgan," I said, "I have an idea."

The gladiator crowd was screaming in my brain as
I ran onto the porch. I whammed on the big, carved
door with my fist. Were Simon and his grandma in
there hiding?

I stomped down the steps and around the house, under the stone lion tongues. "Come on," I yelled.

"I have to keep the dog out here," Morgan called. "Simon's grandma doesn't like him."

The backyard was a tangle of sticks and branches. Some might have blown down in yesterday's winds. Some had obviously been there a long time. Simon could be holding Midnight captive in this mess.

Morgan, help me! But she always had stuck up for Simon.

Branches poked. Too late I saw I was stepping into a spiderweb, all beautiful and awful, too. I slapped at it wildly, trying to get it off me.

At the back of the yard was a slab of cement where a doghouse or something used to be. I saw a tiny sign stuck on one of the trees. ANGEL HOUSES, it said in crooked writing. ANGELS WELCOME.

I knelt down. Tiny houses were lined up on the cement slab. One had a dome made out of sticks and bark and a round bed made out of pebbles and moss. I saw berries and feathers and brown troll head pods.

Behind the dome house was a tent made out of leaves, with a twig ladder leaning against its side, and a table made from a shell resting on four green berries.

Everywhere sat teeny things. Lanterns that were really some kind of seed with a papery shell, all fluttery and transparent. A green bug carcass, shiny in the sun.

Simon must hope his angel mom or dad would visit him. Where *were* all the angels anyway?

Another house in a hollow log. It had a loft, up a tiny ladder, with mushroom drums. A weird secret world.

For a fizzy minute I stood with my hands on my hips. One kid lived here, and the kid had hidden the houses for a reason.

I finally had the power to smite Simon.

CHAPTER 46

૭ᳱ

The Power
to Smite Simon

I put out my foot and poked the dome with my toe. Someone a few streets over was calling for a kid or a dog. Something rustled softly. "Kitty, kitty?" I called.

No answer. Maybe a snake.

I had Simon now. Next time he'd come back here . . . holding a feather or shell or something . . .

Maybe I should jump on the houses. It would take a few seconds to turn everything into mush.

Or with a good kick, that tiny forest of pinecones and tiny fake canoes would explode.

Or, better plan:

1. Run to my house and get a camera.

2. Show everyone at Sunday School.

3. Listen to them mock Simon.

Too bad I wouldn't be around very long to see how he liked his own medicine. Morgan would stick up for him, but it wouldn't be enough. Even when he was scooching around with a cane in his old age, Oakwood folks would say, "There. That's the one."

Wait. People were already saying that.

"There. That's the kid whose dad got in that freaky accident."

Maybe Simon threw rocks and eggs and water balloons at us because he couldn't throw them at God directly.

I started back. Something stickery grabbed my hair, and I had to jerk my head to get loose. That spiderweb was a hanging glob now. The house looked at me with shiny blink-at-me windows.

I went around the corner. *Don't look up at the creepy lions.* Now I couldn't stand it that maybe someone was home. Simon . . . breathing fog rings on the glass. "What's taking so long?" Morgan called.

Maybe she already knew about the angel houses. She'd tell Simon I was there. They'd dismantle everything and say I was having fake visions. It would be some pretty good revenge on me.

"Come on!" Morgan said. "I have an idea for your cat."

I reached the gate. "You do?"

"You know how Bob-Silver tracks down small animals?" She pushed the gate open for me. "I wonder if anyone has ever tried to use a K-nine to find a cat."

"Did you ask your mom?"

"I didn't want her to say it was impossible."

I considered. Bob-Silver? "Do you know anything about how to do it?"

"Do you have something with your cat's scent?" she asked.

I pulled out the green jingling mouse.

"Mom once told me she wasn't sure if his nose could tell the difference between small animals or if they all smell the same to him."

Midnight H. Cat definitely had her own unique smell. But would Bob-Silver think so? "I'm sorry," I blurted out.

"For what?"

I couldn't get words out. The tree house? Sorry that my grandma left and broke your grandma's heart? Sorry about hogging your mom? "Sorry about your dad," I heard myself say. "I'm sure Great-aunt Dorcas is wrong about him."

"Mom says he won't ever come live with us." Morgan kicked the sidewalk. "I want him to, though. When he gets out."

"Maybe he will." One thing I'd learned in Oakwood is that you prepare for something and it doesn't happen and then you don't prepare for something and it does.

"Sit," Morgan said to Bob-Silver. "Do you want to work?"

CHAPTER 47

ༀ

Psychic Bob-Silver

Bob-Silver wiggled like crazy, and his eyes said, *Yes, yes, please*. He and TJ sure thought work made the living sweet.

Morgan brought the toy mouse up under the dog's nose. "Take scent." His ears went forward. "Are you ready?"

He looked at her as if he were saying, *Of course*.

Dogs were that way. They thought they could do anything, just like fifth graders.

"Search," Morgan said.

Bob-Silver started off immediately. "He could be

following Midnight H. Cat's particular scent," I said.

"Maybe." She was too calm—like her mom.

Mr. Garcia was hosing off a muddy string of Christmas lights that must have been in his basement. He lifted his hand to say hello.

I was feeling impressed—until Bob-Silver got his paws up on a tree trunk and I saw the squirrel. "Leave it," Morgan said.

Immediately he found something worse. A random cat. Sitting on a porch.

"Go for it," Morgan told him.

"Why?" I asked.

"If he identifies that cat, we'll know he can't tell the difference between cats."

As Bob-Silver got close, the cat jumped up and hissed. Bob-Silver trotted right back. "Good," Morgan said. "His body language tells us he knows this isn't the cat he was searching for." She glanced at me. "So . . . that's *good*. You can look hopeful."

I wanted to look hopeful. But even a K-9 couldn't uncover a cat that a tornado had whirled off and spit out far away. And by now I could see he was definitely heading toward my house. I'd poked over every inch there.

I needed a psychic dog.

At the tree in our front yard, Bob-Silver halted. His nose twitched as he swung his head from side to side. "He smells something," Morgan said.

"No good." I made smoochy sounds to try to get the dog's attention. Of course Midnight's smell was going to be all over the house and yard. "We're wasting time."

Bob-Silver refused to be distracted. He led us right to the big pile of boards in our backyard. "That's the old shed that collapsed." I rubbed the dog's ear. "She couldn't be there. I've called and called. Why wouldn't she meow?"

"Yeah." Morgan shook her head.

"I looked all around that pile a hundred times."

Bob-Silver whined. He scratched at a mossy log. "Leave it," I said.

"Wait." Morgan bent over. "Shouldn't we at least try his idea?"

I picked up a board. Bugs scuttled everywhere. "Look at Bob-Silver's body language." Morgan got down on her knees. "I wish I could see under that pile."

"I'll get a flashlight," I said. My heart went *thump-thump*. My brain said, *Quit it! It can't be.*

A few minutes later I was back, flat on my belly, with the thin flashlight beam glinting on something shiny. Was it eyes?

"Get my dad!" I shouted.

CHAPTER 48
༺໐༻

Always Two,
Always Together

As Morgan ran off, I lay on my stomach, smelling the dark, wet dirt and trying to keep the flashlight steady in case it was Midnight H. Cat. In case she could see the light. *Please, please, please.* That's all I could think.

I stretched my hand as far as I could and rested it on one of the boards. My thumb hurt. A splinter? An old blister?

Thud. Thud. Thud.

Please. Please. Please.

Once in Colorado I'd flopped like this on the floor

of my tent, making flashlight patterns on the wall, feeling my heart thud against the earth. Just like that time, every second seemed to be big and fat and slow.

Suddenly my dad came rushing around the corner with Mr. Garcia and Mr. Yoder and Mrs. Miller, and I scrambled to my knees.

"Scooch over, honey," Dad said. "Better yet, run in and get a towel."

I leaped up. Now the seconds whistled by. Back door locked. Race around the house. "What are you doing?" I called as I ran by Morgan. She pointed to Bob-Silver to say she didn't want him to freak out my cat.

If it *was* my cat.

Jump the stairs two at a time. Fling my muddy shirt in a corner. Grab a clean one. Grab a towel. Pull the shirt on while I squeaked back down the stairs.

When I got panting back to the yard, Mom was there, holding Isabella. I saw Mr. Garcia toss aside a board. "There," he said. I pushed between Dad and Mr. Yoder and leaned in to see. Midnight H. Cat. Huddled. Shaking.

Mr. Garcia took the towel, bent over and wrapped it around my cat and lifted her out—almost like when Dad rescued her the first time.

"Midnight?" I whispered. I didn't dare reach a finger toward her. In case she was hurt or in shock.

We all glanced at each other. No one seemed to be sure what to do next.

Then Mrs. Miller came rushing up followed by a woman who said, "I'm a vet. Can I help?" I looked into her kind eyes and let out a big whoosh of breath.

Was my cat hurt badly? Was she in pain?

Thud, thud, thud. I walked all draggy shoes behind Mr. Garcia, who carried Midnight H. Cat gently into the house and laid her on the table. "See you soon," he said with a squeeze to my shoulder.

Everyone stepped back to give us room, and the house was suddenly so quiet I heard a fly buzzing.

The vet gave me a steady smile. "Keep her as calm as you can while I check her over."

I stroked Midnight's whiskers and ears and prayed, *Help.* Even without looking, I knew Dad and Mom and Isabella were standing just behind my shoulder, silently watching. "Mae and I called and called around that pile of boards," I said.

"I've seen it with lots of cats." The vet gently moved one back leg and then the other. "They crawl in someplace close to home and stay completely mum even when their owners are searching a few steps away." Her hands moved up and down. "I don't think she has any cuts or broken bones. Just needs a little time and a smidge of loving to be right as rain."

She helped me tuck Midnight H. Cat carefully inside the cat carrier.

That evening a gaggle of people gathered at the church to put things back in the basement: the table, the cook stove, spoons and knives and shovels and rakes and garbage cans and cleaning supplies. I knew their names and faces now. People like Mrs. Miller, who didn't hold Sunday School against me, and Mr. Garcia and Mae and Slurpee and Noah and Chad and

Kylee and Mrs. Yoder and of course the great-aunts and Cousin Caroline and Morgan.

Sort of like a bunch of friends.

When only Stuckys and Nickels were left, Dad said, "I have a big pot of bean soup. Come help us eat it."

Great-aunt Dorcas said, "I can tell you my sister and I need to get ourselves to home and clean up and stay *put* for twelve hours," but Cousin Caroline and Morgan said they would drive Bob-Silver to the farm and come back. It didn't take long before they walked into the house with rolls and lavender honey.

So there we were, sitting around the table, holding hands for the blessing. I couldn't stop looking at Mom and Isabella, in their chairs as if they'd never left.

While we ate, Cousin Caroline and Morgan explained their ideas for the Lavender Festival and a booth at the farmers' market. I definitely wanted it all to work, even though I wouldn't be around to see. I wanted the goat to get big enough to give milk for cheese. I wanted Morgan to even get her horse someday.

Dad put down his spoon and gave us a significant

look. "I appreciate everyone's efforts while I was here." He cleared his throat. "Whatever church I'm in, I don't expect my family to be perfect so everyone will think I'm a great father and husband and nephew." He paused and stared at his plate. "By the way, I don't expect myself to be perfect either."

"Uh-*huh*," Isabella said. "You are."

"Except for your bean soup," I said.

"You know," Dad said, "this bean soup is even better than when I made it." He grinned at me.

I reached for the rolls. "Nice try."

Dad treated us all to his rhinoceros laugh.

Later, while Mom and Dad went upstairs to put Isabella to bed, Cousin Caroline said, "Leave the dishes to Morgan and me and go love up your cat." So I sat on the front steps with the porch light on and Midnight in her carrier beside me. I was thinking about the angel houses I wasn't going to destroy.

Why not? I could hardly figure it out.

Maybe it was because Morgan had every reason to get back at me and she didn't. Maybe it was because small towns are like spiderwebs, and I didn't want to start new things jangling.

I touched one stiff whisker through the carrier door.

Maybe it was what Dad said about our inner jumbles. Maybe it was the teeny tiny baby step of forgiveness, even though I didn't ask for any forgiveness to come along. Maybe old Isabella was right, and it was God in my stomach.

The door opened behind me. Morgan. She smelled like dog, but Midnight didn't even stir, which meant she was really worn out.

"Thanks," I said.

"Yep."

"No, really. You saved my cat." I glanced at Morgan. "I was the one who ruined your tree house. I'm very sorry. It was an accident," I added quickly.

She nodded. "I should have invited you up anyway. It was—you know—awkward."

I looked up at the first stars, and the weight floated off like flies.

Once Katherine, my grandmother, stood in the farmhouse with her suitcase. Morgan's grandma stood there, too. *Always two, always together.* Once sisters had huddled in the cellar with a tornado on the way. Now only feelings were left.

Morgan and I had feelings ahead of us still.

Dad and Cousin Caroline came out, and the three of them walked down the steps. Morgan waved as she got into the car. Even if I were staying in Oakwood, maybe Morgan and I never would have gotten to be a team. She was a sixth grader now. And all the cousins and aunts and great-aunts and first cousins once removed—the whole town of Oakwood—it all wasn't going to stop being a mess anytime soon.

So it was weird that I felt sad.

CHAPTER 49

〇〇

Where Did
All the Angels Go?

When the car drove away, Dad came back and sat
beside me on the porch with buzzing sounds all
around us. Cousin Caroline had said cicadas lived in
the soil for years, sucking on tiny roots, until their
special year came, and then a million of them could
fill up an acre just like that. I knew they wouldn't
bite me because I didn't intend to fake them out by
pretending to be a tree.

I wondered if Dad's arm was hurting and if he was
still upset with me for anything, but all he said was,
"How are *you*?"

All sympathetic.

"I miss Grandpa and Grandma and Colorado," I said.

"I do, too." He sounded completely sincere.

"Does God have power?" I burst out. "Or not? Why did God create tornadoes? Why doesn't God stop people from being enemies and burning down churches?"

Dad wrinkled his nose thoughtfully. "I guess God pretty much leaves some things to us to decide and figure out."

"But an angel shut the mouth of the lions when Daniel was in their den. Now there are disasters *everywhere*! Not just Kansas either. Where did all the angels go?"

He shook his head. "I know what you mean. Big mystery."

I slumped over. Mysteries were a *misery.*

"There are a lot of big certainties, too," Dad said.

I touched a bit of Midnight H. Cat's fur stuck to the porch.

"There's love everywhere," Dad said. "And the Bible says flat out that God is love. So maybe—even in the disasters—our job is to look for love. And *be* love."

Jericho said God needed people's hands. If God was in beautiful and good things, I'd seen God in Kansas a few times. Chickens and emus. The pond. And lavender, even with the bees. Also dogs. Probably it was going to turn out that dogs like TJ and Bob-Silver were the angels who were still around.

Dad squeezed me with his good arm. "The Building and Grounds Committee says there's some wind damage. Old church like that."

I waited. He didn't say anything else. I said, "You want to stay here and help fix it up, don't you? Even if a bunch of people disagree with you and don't listen to your sermons and feel like everything should go their way."

"Do you think I should?"

I leaned against him. "Yes."

"I might, then. Are you going to go to school?"

"Do you think I should?" I asked.

"Yes."

"I might, then."

We went inside, and I climbed up the squeaky stairs with Midnight H. Cat and put her carefully onto the bed in the pink room. After I kissed Mom and Dad good-night, I crawled in between the covers of my bed for the first time and switched off the lamp and the light flew out of the air.

In the dark it wasn't a pink room anymore. It was my room in my temporary house, and after a few minutes I could see big green eyes at the end of my bed, Midnight H. Cat watching to make sure I wasn't going anywhere, making sure Anna was here.